CHRISTMAS WISHES IN HOLLY WREATH

A SWEET CHRISTMAS BILLIONAIRE ROMANCE

RACHAEL ELIKER

ISBN (e-book) 978-1-949876-41-3

ISBN (print) 978-1-949876-42-0

Library of Congress Reference Number 1-10105121937

❀ Created with Vellum

FROM THE BACK COVER

She's happy with small town life. He left without ever looking back. A visit home for Christmas just might make him change his mind.

Katie Holloway is content in Holly Wreath, the only place that's ever been home. The only downside? The dating pool is drying up. When her best friend's older brother comes back to town, she decides this Christmas, there's no better time to finally let him know she's had a crush on him since grade school.

Though Will Ryan plans on getting in and out of Holly Wreath quickly, he reconsiders when he sees his little sister's best friend for the first time in a long time. Katie's grown into the woman he thought didn't exist anymore.

Will isn't in such a hurry to leave and Katie is hoping her Christmas wish comes true, but the unexpected arrival of Will's ex complicates things. Choices have to be made, and neither of them wants to spend the holiday with heartache.

GET YOUR FREE BOOK

Keep in touch with Rachael via her weekly newsletter, and
receive your free book.

Visit www.RachaelEliker.com for details.

For all those who are angels to others each Christmas season.

CHAPTER 1

"**Y**ou ask her," Katie heard whispered behind her back.

"No. *You.*"

Glancing over her shoulder, Katie saw the Stanleys had taken a seat in the corner booth at Holly Wreath's only diner, hiding their prying eyes behind open menus. The second Katie met their gaze, they looked down, pretending to decide what they were going to get. She lowered her eyes, she reciprocated, acting like she hadn't heard them as she focused on her crossword puzzle, but she'd eaten there often enough and at the same time as them to know they always ordered the usual. Two fried eggs with a side of wheat toast and black coffee for Lester, while his wife, Delores, liked to indulge her sweet tooth with a short stack of blueberry pancakes smothered in maple syrup and a cup of apple juice that she dumped a package of sugar into, and not the fake kind.

Taking a swig of orange juice, she closed her eyes to search her brain. What was the French name of Santa Claus, eight letters, starting with a P? Her eyes flicked open, and she grinned, leaning over her newspaper.

Père Noël

She even remembered the accents in the right places. Her high school French teacher would have been so proud.

Finishing up her fruit and yogurt parfait, Katie stacked her dishes and cleaned up her spot, going so far as to wipe up any water drips with her napkin. Her mother would never let her leave an eating establishment without first tidying up to make it easier on whoever was doing the table busing. Mom had been a waitress for as long as Katie could remember, and Katie knew all the restaurant patron faux pas a person could commit. More than one evening was spent listening to Mom recount her shift through gritted teeth when someone particularly rude came in, making life hard for her.

"I'm not getting paid enough to clean up after pigs," she'd say.

Katie made sure she wasn't ever thought of as a pig.

A pair of figures approached and stood silently, watching her do her crossword, but Katie was too engrossed in her puzzle to look up. It wasn't until one of them cleared the gravel out of their throat that she noticed. Katie jumped in her seat at the intrusion. Looking up, she was met with the smiling faces of both the Stanleys.

"Lester. Delores." Katie scooted her dishes out of the way and clasped her hands. She gave them a pleasantly genuine smile. It was going to be entertaining, whatever they had to say. Katie could recognize a scheming elderly couple if ever she saw one. "How are you doing today?"

Whatever they'd been gossiping about would come up in conversation whether she tried to avoid it or not. Holly Wreath, Wyoming was small enough that speculating about others was often a favorite pastime of its residents since not much else exciting beyond the Christmas festival seemed to happen. Katie didn't mind. She'd had enough surprises in her life that she didn't care for any more.

2

"Fantastic," Lester said. He shoved his hands into the pockets of his khakis. "It's nice to see the sun out. Finally."

Katie glanced out the window and appreciated the bright sunlight that was unimpeded by the gray clouds that had settled over the town for the past week. Mother Nature hadn't even had the decency to bring some snow, which always put Katie in the mood for Christmas. "Very true. I feel like I can endure the worst winter Wyoming has to offer as long as I have a dose of sunshine once in a while."

"You just wait until you get to be our age." Delores patted her soft hand over Katie's. "Every time winter comes, my joints ache like they're rusted. Not even sunshine does much to lift my spirits."

"I'm terribly sorry. Have you been to see Dr. Woodhull? Maybe she can prescribe something to take the edge off," Katie suggested. "Or maybe you're going to be one of those couples who snowbird down to Florida every year."

Delores huffed out a laugh. "Christmas without a hint of snow? I don't think so. That would be so...unnatural."

Lester kept the conversation moving as he abruptly changed topics. "How's the planning for your Christmas luncheon going?"

Katie released the sigh of relief that she'd been anxiously holding in her lungs. That's what they wanted to ask her about? It was benign compared to what some other grandparent figures in town were bold enough to ask her. She loved older people, loved hearing their stories, and gleaning from their wisdom, but the number of times she was questioned about her dating life was astounding. A person would think she was constantly on the prowl for a husband when she was perfectly content taking it slow. She was only twenty-two after all. Basically still wet behind the ears.

A proud smile spread across Katie's face as she thought about her charitable efforts. She did well enough for herself as a receptionist at the dentist, but when she volunteered to head up an event meant to provide a hearty Christmas meal to those in town who might not otherwise have a place to go, she felt like a whole new door had been opened to her. She found great satisfaction in helping others. The lives she'd be able to touch would grow exponentially.

"Things are really coming together," Katie answered. "I still have to find a location big enough to fit everyone that's RSVP'd already, but I have faith that everything will fall into place. The important thing is that I think I've got most of the food covered. The community has really stepped up with donations. Now it's just a matter of being organized the week of to make sure I can get all the cooking done in time. I don't suppose anyone would enjoy raw turkey or cold ham with their mashed potatoes and stuffing."

The Stanleys chuckled and Delores said, "Well, we're looking forward to it. It's been far too long since we've had a proper Christmas meal. I haven't been able to muster the energy to do all that work for the two of us."

"I hope it lives up to your expectations then." Katie took a sip of the water out of her secondary glass she'd asked the waitress to bring and got out her credit card. Eyeing the clock above the kitchen entrance, she needed to get going if she was going to make it to work on time unless she wanted to have to run.

"I like cold ham, so you won't have any complaints from me." Lester rubbed his belly.

"I'll remember that, and promise there'll be more than enough to go around," Katie said. "I'll be baking round the clock beforehand to make sure I get everything done."

"Just don't be afraid to ask for help." Delores looked over the top rim of her glasses. "No one expects you to be able to pull it off all on your own."

"Right," Katie agreed, keeping the gnawing worry to

herself that doing it all might be exactly what happened. With such a close-knit, family-oriented town as Holly Wreath, everyone she'd asked to volunteer already had commitments with their own kin.

Pushing her smile wider to disguise her concern, Katie reassured them. "Don't you worry. One way or another, I promise a scrumptious, hearty, home-cooked meal for everyone who's able to make it."

Lester's blue-gray eyes twinkled, and a wry smile tugged at his mouth. Katie's mouth went dry. She'd seen that look before and knew exactly what was coming—her love life. "And what about the Holly Wreath Christmas Festival? I suspect you have young men lined up and down the street, ready to ask you to the social."

Katie dropped her chin down to her chest. *That's* what they were whispering about earlier. Wagging her pointer finger at them, she furrowed her brow. "Maybe I need to go into fortune-telling because I had a feeling the social was going to come up."

"Such a pretty, sweet girl like you shouldn't be missing a party like the social," Delores said with an innocent shrug.

"So? Do you have a special beau who's going to take you?" Lester asked. "If you don't, there are plenty of gentlemen that I would be happy to point in your direction."

Katie pushed a crumb toward her pile of dishes. "Don't worry about me. I've been too busy with planning the Christmas meal that I haven't even been able to give the social a second thought."

Delores frowned and shook her head. "You shouldn't miss out on the joys of youth because you're helping others."

"Life's all about balance," Lester said.

The Stanleys' interrogation unleashed a torrent of emotions in Katie that she masterfully kept tucked away behind a prim smile. She appreciated their concern and encouragement that she should enjoy life to the fullest, but in truth, it wasn't that she didn't want to go. She'd dated most men in town that were her age, and no one had really sparked her interest. Her dates had been too weird or filled with too much drama. One guy was very into traditional roles for men and women and had asked her point-blank on their first date how many children Katie thought she could handle. She made sure he knew not to call back for a second date.

Katie remembered what it was like to feel that exciting attraction to a guy, but the one she'd pined after her whole school life had up and moved away after he graduated, and almost never came back to Holly Wreath. When he did, Katie barely saw him. He wasn't there to visit her. It was hard for the other men she'd dated to hold a candle to the man who she'd let hold her heart for as long as she could remember.

Of course, he had barely acknowledged her existence beyond being his little sister's best friend. That had certainly put a damper on things.

It wouldn't be the first time that she reminded herself that she might as well move on and leave the ridiculous fantasies back in high school where they belonged.

"You are so right. I could use a healthy dose of balance myself." Katie picked up her coat and slipped her arms in. Digging out a piece of gum from her pocket, she unwrapped it and popped it in. "I tell you what. If someone asks me to go, I promise I'll consider their offer."

Lester snapped and pointed a finger at Katie. There was an idea brewing in his head and, if she had to guess, it was going to have something to do with setting her up. She had to give him credit for being quick on the draw. "Say, why don't you go with Timothy?"

Katie nearly choked on her gum. "Timothy? As in—"

"Our grandson," Lester said without a hint he was joking.

Pressing her lips into a thin white line so she didn't laugh —or cry—Katie asked, "How old do you think I am, Lester?"

Confused, Lester looked over at his wife, whose shoulders were shaking with suppressed laughter. "I dunno. Eighteen? I figured you for a senior in high school."

"If I was still in high school, I'd be there right now, not getting ready to go work at the dentist's office," Katie teased.

"I have no doubt Timothy would love to take her so he could brag to all his friends," Delores said as she held back her own laugh, "but I don't think we should subject our dear Katie to that kind of humiliation. Timothy is only seventeen."

Lester's bushy gray eyebrows scrunched together. "How old are you then?"

"Twenty-two. Celebrated this past September." Katie pulled her glossy brunette ponytail out from under the collar of her coat. "I've been a full-blown adult for the past year, and if I don't want to get in some serious trouble, I'm going to have to pass on taking Timothy."

"Yes, I see," Lester said awkwardly while his cheeks turned rosy. At least he had the sense to be embarrassed.

The waitress came and took Katie's payment, and she was sure to leave a generous cash tip under her water glass. Katie scooted to the end of her booth, ready to leave the moment her check made it back to the table. "Besides, I have it on good authority that Timothy is taking a pretty redhead from school to the tree lighting. I'd hate to be causing any trouble for him by having a girl on the side."

Lester's eyebrows went the opposite direction and shot halfway up his forehead. "He is?"

"Told me last week when he was checking in at the dentist," Katie said. "He's very excited."

"Well, good." Lester's eyes lit up again. "What about—"

"Would you look at the time?" Delores linked arms with Lester and towed him toward the door. "We're going to be late for Bingo if we don't get going, and I am not about to be beaten by Nancy again because I showed up late."

The knot of stress that had burrowed itself in Katie's shoulders left with Lester, and she thanked the waitress as she brought back her card and receipt. She stood up and buttoned her coat, double-checking her booth that she hadn't left anything behind.

Katie heard the doorbell ding as she tied her scarf around her neck, and Katie glanced over to see Charlotte breeze through the door.

"Katie!" she squealed.

The entire dining area turned to look at Katie's best friend, though Charlotte was blissfully unaware that she was the center of attention, however briefly.

Charlotte was comfortable in the limelight in a way Katie had never understood. She preferred playing second fiddle to Charlotte, and maybe that's why their friendship had always worked so well. They were polar opposites, complimenting each other, though their love of chocolate, romance movies, and humor largely overlapped.

"Hey, Charlotte." Katie accepted a quick hug from her friend. "What are you doing here this morning? I thought you were working at the salon today."

"Nah. I had one grumpy guy earlier, but no one else is scheduled to come in for two more hours, so I thought I'd get a bite to eat."

Katie glanced sideways out to the street where Charlotte's Porsche was parked and smirked to herself. It was an entirely impractical car to be driving in winter but, in a nutshell, that was Charlotte. A bit unreasonable for the sake of being flashy, but still the kindest person anyone would ever meet. Even working at her own hair salon was a public service. She didn't need to have a job at all, thanks to her well-off brother's generosity, but nobody could deny she was the town's best hairstylist. Probably in the whole state. It didn't matter if her customers were little old ladies getting their white hair cropped short or a dewy-eyed teenage girl having her hair fixed for prom, Charlotte could make them look amazing.

"That must be nice, to be your own boss," Katie said wistfully.

Charlotte tossed her silky hair. "Just because my brother set me up for the rest of my life doesn't mean I don't think work is important for a person. I just don't like to sit around and twiddle my thumbs, waiting for someone to walk in. Unless, of course, you want to come to the salon so I can play with your hair."

Charlotte looked innocent enough, but Katie's right eyebrow vaulted upward. "I know you want to go all scissor-crazy on my hair, but I like what you've been doing with it already."

Pouting, Charlotte fingered the ends of Katie's hair. "It does look like you could use a trim. I see some split ends."

"What? One? I was in less than a month ago to let you cut it. I know you're trying to trick me. One minute, you'll be trimming my perfectly acceptable hairstyle, the next, I'm going to be platinum blonde or something. I wouldn't put it past you to give me a big blue streak, too." Katie playfully narrowed her eyes and poked Charlotte's shoulder. "I'm on to you."

Feigning hurt, Charlotte pressed her hand to her chest. "Me? Scheming? That's a knife in the back right there. Et tu, Katie?"

Katie slipped her purse strap over her shoulder. "Are you sure you're not up to something? I know you well enough to know the expression on your face wasn't all innocent."

"Not up to something. Just happy. Though someday, you have to promise me you'll let me give you a total makeover.

Trust me. I'll make everything from your cheekbones to your legs look fantastic."

"My legs?" Katie scrunched her nose. "Call me skeptical, but I'm not sure what changing my hair and applying more makeup will do for any of my limbs."

"You'd be a believer if you let me try."

Katie let her eyes roll. "Other than the prospect of chopping off my perfectly good hair, what else is making you so happy?"

Charlotte squealed and did a little dance. "The Holly Wreath Christmas Social."

A groan overpowered Katie. "Please don't tell me you're going to try and set me up with someone, too."

"No. Why would I?" Charlotte asked, her face contorted with confusion. "Are the matchmakers out?"

"Big time." Katie made sure the Stanleys were long gone so they wouldn't overhear. "Lester suggested I go with Timothy."

"Timothy? As in their grandkid? The one who sometimes helps at my parents' produce stand?"

"Yeah."

Charlotte held a hand over her mouth as laughter sputtered from her. "Isn't he like, twelve?"

"Seventeen. Almost a man, yet not even close."

"Oh, Katie." Charlotte patted at the tears in the corner of her eyes while clutching her stomach. "I'm sorry. That must've been horrifying."

"It'll make a good story for my imaginary grandchildren that someday I may or may not have. But seriously, why is everyone so concerned about whether or not I'm going with someone? Can't I be happily unattached? Maybe I'll go by myself. It's the twenty-first century, after all."

Charlotte shrugged. "Meddling and knowing everyone else's business kind of comes with living here."

"I know." Katie sighed. "I take it the reason you're so giddy about the social is because you *are* attached to someone."

Charlotte looked like she was about to explode, shaking her hands and squealing as she danced in place. When she couldn't take it any longer, she said in a stage whisper, "Harvey asked me to go with him. *Finally.*"

Katie's jaw unhinged. "You're kidding me! How'd he work up the courage? He's the quietest, shyest guy I think I've ever met."

"Yeah," Charlotte said starry-eyed. "I've been dropping hints like crazy that I wanted him to ask and, last night after I cut his hair, I thought he was going to pass out because it so happens, he's been trying to ask me to go with him for like, seven months. He had to man up but once I said yes, he was so relieved."

"Well, you are a force to be reckoned with. Beautiful, successful, witty, taller than your everyday giant."

"Hey, now. Watch it." Charlotte poked her manicured nail into Katie's shoulder. "I might squish your average-sized hiney and then we'll see if you make fun of my height."

"As fun as it is to tease you about some of the short men you've dated, I'm very glad that Harvey is tall. So tall I daresay you'll be able to wear your freakishly high heels and still not be taller than him."

Charlotte rubbed her hands together. "Is it stupid to admit that's one of the things I'm looking forward to the most?" She giggled behind her hands, and Katie joined her.

"Well, I'm happy for you. You deserve it."

Charlotte tilted her head toward the counter and pulled out her wallet. Giving the waitress a crisp twenty and telling her to keep the change, she pointed to two large apple-stuffed fritters from the display. "So do you. You know, finding a date would put an end to everybody's matchmaking pretty quickly. That would show them."

"Easier said than done," Katie countered. "I'm fairly positive there is no one in the whole of Holly Wreath that I can think of who'd make a suitable date. Everyone I've gone out with lately was a big fat no."

Charlotte took a bite of her fritter, licking the flaky crumbs off her rosy red-lipsticked lips. "What about that guy who wanted to talk kids on the first date?"

Katie put her head down on the counter, hiding her mortification by boxing herself in with her arms. "Don't even remind me. I'm still scarred from that date. And I didn't even get a free meal. He forgot his wallet and I had to pay."

Starting on another giggling fit, Charlotte poked Katie's side, nearly hard enough to knock her off her seat. "Seriously, Katie. He could have been the one. You will make some adorable babies, regardless of who it's with."

"Gross," Katie grumbled. "I have nothing against men with thinning hair, but he was like thirty and already had a greasy comb-over. Shouldn't physical attraction be one of the first signs that you might be compatible with someone?"

Charlotte took another bite of her fritter while she thought. "Maybe we need to start looking for your soulmate outside of the confines of Holly Wreath."

Drumming her fingernails on the counter, Katie let her thoughts stray to the one boy she'd had a crush on for as long as she could remember. He was a man now, and he was definitely long gone from Holly Wreath, leaving her with some serious, unresolved pining. He'd fit the bill since Katie would have to look far, far outside of Holly Wreath to find him.

Charlotte leaned over and nudged Katie with her shoulder. "You're thinking about your mystery man, aren't you?"

"What?" Katie snapped out of her gratifying morning reverie. "I don't know what you're talking about."

"I'm talking about the guy that you've had a crush on for ages, but because your mouth is basically a steel trap when you want to keep a secret, nobody's ever found out who it is."

"I was not." Except she was. She was thinking of the wave in his hair when it got too long, how intense his hazel eyes were, how his broad shoulders barely fit under the hood of the sports car he restored in high school. "Besides. Even if I was, he's not anywhere in the vicinity and probably has no idea the Holly Wreath festivities are happening at all."

Charlotte's face lit up and she squealed. "You just admitted that there is a mystery man! Tell me about him. How did you meet? What color is his hair? Is he tall, too?"

Katie couldn't believe she'd slipped. Flicking her wrist and looking at her imaginary watch, she said, "Gee. Look at the time. It was nice chatting, but I'm going to be late for work if I don't get going."

Katie heard the front doorbell ding again and she had to blink to make sure she wasn't still dreaming. He'd matured so much since she'd seen him in person last but his eyes were still the same. So were the dimples as his gaze met hers and he grinned.

"Hello, Katie. Long time, no see."

CHAPTER 2

The gray cloud that had been hanging over Will since he'd gotten into town the night before dissipated the instant he saw Katie Holloway. He hadn't been particularly excited about the thought of visiting Holly Wreath, even if it was to help out family, and he'd let it affect his mood. The trip back felt like a step down from the high life he'd been living in Austin. He'd even been away long enough that the cold of an early Wyoming December seemed to be seeping straight into him. His family had teased him relentlessly when he arrived in his rental car, bundled up in everything from gloves to a knit hat when they came outside to greet him in little more than light jackets.

Katie's mouth hung open as he sauntered over, but she recovered quickly and replaced it with a smirk. "Will Ryan? Is that you?"

"In the flesh." Will sat down on the counter-height chair, sandwiching Katie between him and his sister.

"Well, I hardly recognized you." Katie didn't hide that she was studying his face and he took the opportunity to reciprocate. Though she'd been a cute kid, with a smattering of freckles across her nose and cheeks and wild hair that she never seemed to be able to tame, Katie had matured into a striking woman. How he'd missed that when they were in high school was beyond him, although age had a lot to do with it. Four years between a freshman and senior was a lot. Now? He didn't mind one bit.

Charlotte interrupted and reached over, fussing with her brother's hair. "That's because I made him look good. Whoever cuts his hair down in Austin doesn't know the first thing about blending men's haircuts. It's like he's a new man every time I rescue him."

Will jerked his head away and smoothed his hair back as best he could. "You should know better than anyone how hard it is to find a decent person to cut hair when you move."

Katie clasped her hands on the diner countertop. "I was going to say I hardly recognized you because it's been a long time since I've seen you. In person anyway."

"If you haven't seen me in person, where else have you been seeing me?" Will quirked his eyebrow. "Have you been following me in the tabloids?"

Katie pursed her lips and fought down a blush, which pleased him. He'd always liked teasing her when she'd come over to hang out with Charlotte after school. "It's kind of hard not to. You're on every other website and in every trashy magazine in the checkout lane at the grocery store."

"But the question is, do you pick up those magazines?" Will asked. Katie answered with a roll of her eyes and scoffed but didn't deny it, making Will and Charlotte both laugh. "Huh. I see."

"Give her a break," Charlotte said, wiping up the crumbs from her spot and putting them back on her plate. "She's right. You kind of are everywhere. It's annoying. I want to read my trashy magazines without seeing my brother splashed across every other page."

"I can't help it that the public is fascinated with me." Sitting forward and resting on his forearms, he pointed over to the apple fritter by Charlotte. "Is that for me or are you really hungry?"

"Maybe it's for Katie. She's nice to me," Charlotte sassed.

"No. Oh, no," Katie said, patting her stomach. "I already ate too much as it is. It's all yours, Will."

She slid the plate over to Will before Charlotte could stop her. Taking a monstrous bite, Will smirked. "Katie's nice to me, too."

Will watched Katie from the corner of his eye as she tucked her chin to her chest and pursed her lips. She looked like she was blushing again.

The moment passed and Katie flipped her hair over her shoulder, watching him under her thick lashes. "What brings you back to Holly Wreath anyway? From what Charlotte's told me, she made it sound like you were never going to set foot here again."

"I would've gladly stayed away if I didn't have to come back," Will said flatly. His admission seemed to rub Katie the wrong way, and he could see the hurt in her deep brown eyes, immediately making him regret his choice of words. Why he cared so much surprised him, but he did. "I mean, Holly Wreath is a fine enough town, but if it weren't for my family, it'd definitely be one of those places I'd drive straight through without stopping."

His fumbling correction didn't impress Katie and she frowned at him. "Well, I hope you're doing Holly Wreath proud since probably every woman with a pulse knows you're from here. That's half the world's population right there that thinks you're the gem of our humble settlement."

He chuckled. "Don't worry. I keep my opinions about Holly Wreath to myself for the most part. Besides, the women of the world adore me."

Katie dropped her head and groaned, renewing Will and Charlotte's raucous laughter.

"As much of a jerk as Will pretends to be," Charlotte said, "he's actually come back for a very noble reason."

Furrowing her brow, Katie asked coolly. "Is that so?"

Will poked at the errant flakes of fritters that had fallen from his mouth and onto the counter. "Our parents need help with the harvest this year since they're so far behind. When dad decided to climb a ladder to fix the hayloft door on the barn, he didn't plan on falling off."

"Right," Katie said solemnly. "He tore up his shoulder pretty badly. They still have three-fourths of their corn to bring in."

"It's hard to drive a combine or take the wagon to the grain elevator with one incapacitated arm," Will agreed.

"Right. How is your dad doing?" The way Katie tilted her head and narrowed her eyes ever so slightly struck Will. She genuinely cared about his parents.

"You saw him two days ago," Charlotte pointed out.

"I know." Katie shrugged. "But he had another appointment yesterday, right?"

Charlotte ran her fingers through her glossy hair and checked that her nails were still impeccable. Chipped nail polish was a big no-no. "Not much has changed since Dad's last appointment. Everything is on the mend. Slowly. Mostly Mom is about to go crazy having Dad sitting around at home, messing up her routine."

Will leaned back in his seat and laced his fingers behind his head. "You see our parents regularly?"

Katie looked straightforwardly at Will, and he noticed the immediate uptick of his pulse. The mischievousness gleaming in her eyes only added another layer of depth to her pretty features.

"Maybe I'm their new favorite child since you've become the absentee son," she quipped.

Putting his hands over his chest, Will faked that he'd been struck through the heart. "Wow, Katie. That was harsh. What about Charlotte?"

"Hey, yeah," Charlotte said. "What about me?"

"You and Charlotte are so dramatic." She shrugged nonchalantly. "Sometimes the truth hurts."

Charlotte was laughing loud enough that it embarrassed Will when people looked up and stared. "She got you there, Will. Our parents love Katie. They have for a long time."

"Who wouldn't?" Will watched Katie go beet red. He was going to enjoy harmlessly flirting with Katie. It'd give him something fun to do while he was back.

Will caught himself staring a moment too long at Katie, making Katie fidget, which she tried to hide by letting her hair fall like a curtain around her face, outright blocking him. He was not one to believe in any sort of wild notions that love at first sight existed, especially after he'd had his heart ripped out and stomped on by his last serious girl-friend from Holly Wreath, but Katie intrigued him in a way that none of his flings had, and he'd had plenty of them in Austin.

Not only did Katie speak her mind, she wasn't afraid to give him a good dose of sass, and as far as Will was concerned, anyone who could put up with his sister through her middle school years was a saint. He knew, however, that Katie was off-limits. Not only had he made a home hundreds of miles away and would be returning there as soon as he had the chance, but dating his baby sister's best friend was too risky. If it didn't work out, it'd put Charlotte in the middle of a feud. Will had never mastered the art of amicable breakups.

Charlotte leaned her elbows onto the counter and drummed her fingertips on her chin. "Who, who, who…"

"Who, what?" Katie asked.

Charlotte blinked at Katie's intrusion into her thoughts. "Huh?"

"Either you're wondering about someone, or you're pretending you're an owl, in which case, I have evidence that you've finally cracked." Katie's teasing simper was too cute and Will went to pieces again.

"Oh," Charlotte said breathily. "I was trying to figure out who could take Katie to the Holly Wreath Christmas Social."

The blood left Katie's face and she frowned. "I'd rather have a root canal without novocaine than have this conversation right now."

Charlotte grabbed her wrist with an iron grip to keep her from leaving. "You might want to be careful, working for a dentist and all. They enjoy inflicting pain like that on people."

"No," Katie shook her head. "Dr. Hamilton is not that sinister."

"Says you. That's sure not what it felt like the last time I was in to get a filling." Charlotte pulled aside her lip to show the molar he'd worked on.

Katie pushed her hand away. "Oh, stop. It's not his fault you don't brush your teeth well enough for all the candy you eat."

"Yeah," Will chimed in. "It's not the first cavity you've had."

"That's not the point," Charlotte said. "We're talking about a date for Katie, not my dental health history. If we don't talk about a date for Katie now, she's going to pretend like it never came up and, then, we're going to get nowhere."

"I can't believe they still do the social," Will said.

"Gets bigger and better every year," Charlotte said. "Last

year they hired out an ice sculptor to make a life-sized Santa."

Will whistled. "Wow. That sounds like quite the shindig, what, with ice sculptures and all."

"Shut up." Charlotte reached around Katie to shove her brother but ended up squashing Katie against him. He didn't mind though. Her scent was a mixture of honey and berries with a hint of something spicy...nutmeg? "Just because you've been jaded by big city parties that go on until all hours of the night doesn't mean that we don't know how to enjoy ourselves here. I think you're jealous that you never had a chance to go to one of the socials, since you moved away right after you graduated and it's always been an adults-only party."

"That has to be it," Will said, earning him another smack from his sister. "I think what's surprised me the most is that Katie doesn't have a boyfriend to take her. I thought for sure by now she'd be attached to someone."

Charlotte's eyebrows shot up her forehead, and she gave her brother a wry smile. "Thinking about her availability, are you?"

Will's eyes cut over to Katie and she was looking straight back at him with a slight panic in her expression. "No," he said. "Just thinking aloud, that's all."

Katie pressed her lips together and she gathered her things. "Well, if you must know, the dating pool in Holly Wreath is drying up faster than I care to admit. People our age are pairing off and getting married or have been scratched off the list for being losers."

"Seriously." Charlotte sucked obnoxiously on her straw, trying to get at the last of the ice water in her glass. "You should ask her how many children she thinks she could handle."

Will covered his mouth with his hand, trying to cover his

burst of laughter with a cough. It sounded more like he was being strangled. "Well, Holloway? How many kids *do* you think you'd like to have?"

Katie poked him in the ribs, right in the spot where he was ticklish. He yelped in surprise and the devilish look in her eye was revealing. She knew exactly what she was doing. "He was an outlier, that guy. Not everyone is as bad as Charlotte makes them sound."

Will played with the wrapper from his straw. "So, you haven't found Mr. Right, huh?"

Charlotte had taken to writing down something on a napkin with a pen she'd dug out of her purse. She shook her head, making her hoop earrings move wildly. "Nope. Katie is single and ready to mingle."

Leaning over to see what she was writing, Will realized it was a list of men's names that Charlotte was trying to brainstorm for Katie. As the list grew longer, Will was caught off guard by the stab of jealousy that made his stomach turn sour. What did he care who Katie went with? It's not like he hadn't had his share of dates on the weekends.

When Katie caught on to what Charlotte was doing, she snatched the napkin from her friend and skimmed over it. "Timothy right at the top? Nice."

Ripping the napkin to shreds, Katie ignored Charlotte's protests and tossed the napkin on Charlotte's empty plate. "Look. Since it is apparently bothering the entire town of Holly Wreath that I wasn't going to even go, I'll solve everyone's problems and make an appearance, even though I was going to watch a movie and soak my feet until they looked like prunes."

"You do that every weekend," Charlotte pointed out.

"And?" Raising her nose a notch, Katie dared Charlotte to say another word about it.

"And, I think it's weird that you have your weekends

21

planned out weeks in advance. It wouldn't kill you to get out and have some fun."

"That's precisely why I'm going." Katie straightened her spine. "I'm going to get myself all dolled up, eat their delicious dinner, maybe even dance a little while I'm there."

One side of Will's mouth inched up. He liked seeing Katie assert herself. "Oh, yeah? With who?"

Katie took her lip balm out of her purse and smoothed it over her lips. Will liked the scent and the way it tinted her lips. He blinked and looked away before she caught him staring.

"Nobody," Katie said resolutely. "I'm going to shock every matchmaker in Holly Wreath by going all by myself."

CHAPTER 3

"What was I thinking?" Katie asked aloud. "What *am* I thinking?"

Katie was alone in the chicken coop, but having a flock of hens clucking and scratching around her made speaking seem like she was hashing out her problems surrounded by friends rather than losing her mind, talking aloud to nobody.

Scraping up a pile of soiled straw she'd collected, she tossed it into an old wheelbarrow. At one time it was probably a glossy, striking blue, but it'd been part of the Ryan family farm for who knew how long and had certainly given its best years to them. "I *know* Will is out of bounds. He's my best friend's older brother for crying out loud!"

Katie took a step back and startled a plump black Australorp hen who'd been picking at dropped bits of grain behind Katie's boots. The hen squawked angrily and ran out from underfoot, flapping her wings vigorously as she escaped. Muttering her apology to the ruffled hen, Katie sighed and leaned on her stall fork, speaking directly to the chicken. The black hen's feathers looked iridescent in the sunlight and Katie smiled at the analogy that formed in her head. People might overlook Katie for being plain, but look close enough and they were lucky to get to see her for who she truly was.

"I can't even begin to imagine how mortified Charlotte would be, knowing I'm hankering for Will. I mean, I was searching for a reason to come out here. No woman in her right mind would agree to clean out a chicken coop just to catch a glimpse of the guy she's crushing on."

The hen clucked and watched Katie, her yellow eye trained on her with keen interest. It'd been a couple of days since Will had been back, and she hadn't seen him since she'd turned red in the face as they discussed her love life so cavalierly, wishing the ground would open up and swallow her whole. The only guy she'd ever wanted was sitting right next to her, so close she could practically feel the warmth coming off of him. Still, it wasn't enough. She wanted more of him.

But she couldn't. Not only was he her best friend's brother, he was a big deal in the world. Katie? She was little more than a country bumpkin. He'd become a billionaire before his twenty-fifth birthday when he'd developed the new, hottest wave of social media, while she had only gone to a local community college for a two-year degree. It was so close, she could still live at home with her mom and still drive to class without having to wake up insanely early.

Katie and Will weren't exactly living compatible lives.

Since Will had become such a hotshot, his life had become increasingly public, including his dating. Womanizer wasn't the term Katie would give him, but he certainly had his share of beautiful women clinging to his arm. Their dating lives were also definitely worlds apart.

"I'm not going to risk a lifelong friendship with Charlotte on a whim. No. I'm going to go to the social on my own like I said I would. No more girlish fantasies."

The black hen tilted her head at Katie, making her grin and drop her gaze down to the dusty muck boots she was wearing. Laughing weakly, Katie said, "It's official. I *am* totally crazy. I'm using chickens for free therapy."

Raking up the last of the old bedding, Katie tossed it into the wheelbarrow and brushed her hands on her favorite pair of work jeans. There was a hole in the knee but, otherwise, they were solid and had seen her through lots of hard work.

"Katie?" she heard a voice coming from outside.

Pushing her wheelbarrow out the door, she saw Will and Charlotte's mom approaching with an armful of clean mason jars stacked in a cardboard box.

"Just finishing up with the chicken coop, Mrs. Ryan," Katie said, hoping their mom hadn't overheard Katie talking to her flock.

"You're an angel," she said. "I haven't been able to get to them for a month, with trying to keep on top of everything since Roger's injury. I'm sure they appreciate having a clean place to nest. And remember, it's Carol."

"Right. Carol," Katie said obediently.

"I don't want to keep you. I know what a busy lady you are, especially with the Christmas season approaching. You collect all the eggs the hens laid and take them home with you. I've got some in the fridge that I want to donate to your Christmas dinner. Do you think you could use them?"

"That's very generous of you." Katie took off her gloves and stuffed them in her pockets. Involuntarily, her eyes darted to the back door of the Ryan's white two-story farmhouse, wondering if Will was already out helping his dad with the harvest. The Christmas lights had been hung on the gutters and a large inflatable snowman bobbed in the front yard. It looked like Will had been running through a to-do list since being home. "A person can never have too many eggs when making a Christmas dinner for several dozen people."

"Very good. I'll keep them here for you until you're ready for them."

"Deal." Katie tipped her head at the jars Carol was toting. "What are you doing with those?"

As a tall woman with a strong back, Carol was suited to farm life. Easily shifting the jars to her hip, she pointed to an enormous shed covered in corrugated metal that had been recently built on their property, replacing an old detached garage where Katie used to catch glimpses of Will working on his car. "I was going to finish canning the last of the apple jelly. All the apples I picked this fall are going to go bad if I don't do something with them, and we're all sick of apple pie and applesauce for now. It's probably foolish of me to try to be taking on all this extra work, especially when Roger decided to go and break himself by falling off that darned ladder, but I need a little alone time in my new canning kitchen."

"I was wondering what was inside that enormous building."

Carol chuckled. "A gift from Will. Over the top, for sure, but I can't really complain. The entire thing is insulated and it's big enough for Roger to park all his equipment. Part of it Will and Roger had sectioned off just for me. It's got a brand new stove and fridge and there's enough countertop space that I don't have to shuffle anything around when I'm canning. I do feel a smidgen spoiled."

Katie nodded. "I'm glad to see he's still taking care of his family, even if he hates coming back to Holly Wreath."

"I don't think he hates it," Carol said, "but he didn't leave under particularly happy circumstances, so it's left a bit of a bad taste in his mouth."

"Yeah? I didn't know that."

"Remember Megan Smart?"

It was hard for Katie to speak around the lump lodged in her throat. "His high school girlfriend?" It hurt to say because Katie had never claimed that honor. In fact, Megan had been the only one Will had dated while he lived in Holly Wreath. Back then, he was a one lady kind of guy.

"The very one. A charming gal but she knew how to break hearts and make sure a boy was knocked down for the count. I think that's part of the reason Will has a hard time coming back. It...reminds him of a difficult time of life."

"So he needs some good memories to remind him how amazing Holly Wreath is."

Carol tapped her nose, then pointed to Katie. "I think you're on to something. As much as I appreciate his big, showy gestures, like building a machine shed, I'd rather see him home more often."

Katie grinned stupidly, thinking that she'd like the exact same thing. "I don't want to keep you from canning. Could you use a hand with any of it?"

"You don't have to work today?"

"Nope. I took time off to go pick up some donations later today for the Christmas luncheon around town, but it doesn't matter when I go. Otherwise, I'm a free woman. I'd love to be put to good use and relearn some kitchen skills that I haven't quite mastered yet."

Carol put her hand on her hip and shook her head while grinning at Katie. "If half the people in this world had an ounce of your work ethic, we'd all be better for it."

Katie shrugged. "My offer isn't totally benevolent. I remember canning with my mom and grandma, so it makes me nostalgic when I get the chance to do it again."

The sadness in Carol's expression made Katie regret her choice of words. The look of pity was worse than feeling sad herself because she knew she'd caused another person to feel bad, too. Katie was fine. She'd come to terms with her family history—she really had, but every time she was on the receiving end of one of those looks, it was like reliving those dark days again.

Taking one of the flats of Mason jars off Carol's hands, Katie quickly added, "I've only ever done strawberry jam before, so I'm sure I'll have a thing or two to learn about apple jelly."

Carol nodded, letting the hiccup in their conversation slide without saying anything else, which eased the tightness in Katie's chest.

Katie followed Carol, who opened the door to her second kitchen. On every available inch of counter space were bushels of several varieties of apples, straight from their own orchard.

"Is there anything you don't do?" Katie asked with admiration, leaning against the doorway and tucking her hands into her pockets.

"Careful there, girl. You're gonna make this old cow get a big head."

A peal of laughter soared out of Katie as the back door to the house opened, and Will stepped onto the porch. His hair was disheveled from sleeping, and he reached his arms high over his head, groaning with satisfaction as he stretched.

When he caught Katie's eye, he sent a friendly wave in her direction. Twiddling her fingers toward him, she had to take a deep breath to calm her racing heart. She hoped she wasn't crushing too hard on him that it was obvious to the entire world, but judging by the teasing look in Carol's eye that she'd also seen in Charlotte's, people were going to start guessing pretty quickly.

Will stuffed his feet into a pair of boots and strolled over to the canning kitchen, his arms folded in front of his chest to keep warm against the briskness of the morning. When

Katie realized she was staring straight at his toned biceps, she forced herself to blink and quickly look away, pretending to comb a snarl out of her ponytail with her fingers. She'd never seen a gray t-shirt look so good on a guy, but she couldn't be losing her mind every time she was around him. That would give away her secret all too easily.

"I never pegged you for a late sleeper," Katie said as Will stepped into the kitchen with them. She wasn't about to let Carol direct the conversation, especially if she was catching on to the fact that Katie had been ogling her son.

"It's not often I get to have a break from my regular job, so I'm considering no need for an alarm clock as one of the perks." Will shrugged. "I'm going to take advantage of it as long as I have the chance."

Narrowing her eyes, Katie asked, "I thought farmers were up at the crack of dawn."

"Guess it's good I'm not a farmer," Will said.

"You should probably try while you're here," Katie pointed out. "I thought that was the whole reason you came back."

Will conceded, showing off his dimples in a way that made Katie's heart pitter-patter in her chest all over again. "Fair enough. If it were planting season, I'd be up at the crack of dawn, but since we're harvesting, Dad likes to wait until the sun has burned off the frost so the corn we take to the elevator is as dry as possible. Hence my ability to sleep in."

"You boys aren't going to have much longer before the snow really starts to come in," Carol said, resting a fist right at her waist. "I'm amazed how lucky you've been to not already be trying to plow through those fields with half a foot of snow on the ground already."

"I must be good luck." There were Will's dimples again, making Katie's body react the same way. She was hopeless.

Carol swatted at Will with a folded newspaper she'd had on the countertop. "Didn't I teach you to be humble?"

"Humble doesn't mean you can't recognize your talents," Will shot back.

Carol pursed her lips, but didn't give his ego any more grief.

"Who's watching over things while you're gone?" Katie asked.

Will pushed the jars aside, jumped up onto the island, and folded his arms, giving Katie a fantastic view of the veins running up and down the length of his forearms. "It's been a long time since it was just me and a couple of other programmers working at the company. I don't have to sit there plugging code unless I want to, and if I want to, I can do it from home. Any more, I'm merely the public face of the company."

"Good thing you've got a handsome face," Katie said, laughing.

When she realized that she'd said what she'd been thinking out loud, a splash of icy cold poured over her whole body. Her mouth was going to ruin her if she didn't get it under control.

"Thank you," Will said, his tone dancing with amusement. "See, Ma? Katie can recognize that I'm good at something."

Carol pinched his chin and gently shook his face. "I've always known I made beautiful human beings but that doesn't mean I want you and Charlotte getting big heads over it. I see how many girls' hearts you've broken."

"You read the celebrity gossip magazines, too?" Will made a face at her. "I never really pegged you for that kind of reading material."

"Charlotte has shown me the magazines she has delivered to her salon a time or two when I go in to get my hair done," Carol answered. "I'm not at all opposed to you young people dating around and finding what kind of personalities you're compatible with, but I really don't like you being so cavalier with how you treat your relationships. Your father and I want you to find a nice girl. Like Katie."

The conversation couldn't have gotten awkward any faster than if Katie had blurted out everything that she loved about Will without being prompted.

Will's eyes flashed to Katie, apologizing with his gaze and he picked up a jar, tossing it casually in his hands. She would have kept the connection with him longer—she loved looking at the color of his eyes. It reminded her of wheat fields that were in between lush green and the golden hue right before harvest. "I'd rather not talk about my dating life right now and, I think, neither does Katie."

"I'm just saying, maybe you ought to hang around Holly Wreath a little more often." Carol winked conspicuously at Katie and her already hot skin turned volcanic. It wasn't that Katie didn't want to pursue Will, but she wanted to do it on her own terms. Carol's attempt to hurry things along was mortifying.

"Anyway," Will jumped down and walked over to the apples, picking one and shining it on his t-shirt before taking a massive bite, "is this apple jelly going to be done by dinner?"

Carol snatched the jar from his hand. "You and your stomach. If you aren't careful, you're going to regret eating two helpings at every meal while you're home."

"Then stop cooking so much good food," Will taunted.

Carol sighed at her son's snarkiness. "Are you out here to help me get the canning done, or are you going to twiddle your thumbs when you should be out harvesting? If I can ask for something for Christmas, I'd like this farm back on track sooner rather than later."

"Mom," Will said, dropping his head and chuckling in

exasperation, "I told you. We're working as hard as we can. I've had to help Dad tune up some of his machines since he hasn't done the preseason work because of his shoulder. It's been taking a bit longer than expected."

"Needing parts?" Carol asked. "I can run to town to get them if that's what's holding you up."

Blowing out a breath, Will shook his head. "Nah, it's not that."

"What is it then?" his mother asked.

Will rubbed the back of his neck. "I might be a bit...*lacking* with my mechanics skills lately. Other than changing the oil in my car, there aren't a lot of other chances to turn a wrench where I'm living."

Carol laughed, the same free-spirited one that Charlotte had inherited from her. "Boy, you're going soft sitting behind a computer all day."

Will straightened his shoulders and said, "Not soft. Rusty."

"Right," said Carol. "As much as I'd love to tease you about turning into a city boy, I need to get Katie out of here while the sun's still shining so she can pick up the donations she needs." Carol turned around the kitchen, looking for something. "Oh, shoot. I left my radio in the house. I can't work without music. Hang on. I'll be right back."

Carol left, swinging the door shut as she went. If Katie didn't know any better, a missing radio was all part of her conspicuous matchmaking.

"Donations?" Will asked, his interest piqued. "What for? Wait. Let me guess. You're picking up toothbrush donations so Santa can drop off lame stocking stuffers for kids instead of candy."

Shoving him hard, Katie knocked Will off balance, but he grabbed her wrists to keep himself standing. Her skin tingled under his touch and she loved hearing his lighthearted laughter. It made her mind wander to what things might have been like if Will had stuck around after high school instead of disappearing beyond her reach. She could have worked up the courage to tell him how she felt a long time ago.

At least, maybe she would have. It was still entirely possible that she would have chickened out and would be in the exact same predicament she was currently living.

"William Ryan, I can't believe you!" Katie said sternly.

Laughing, Will held his hands up in surrender and Katie missed his touch. "I'm just kidding."

"Cavities aren't anything to joke about." Katie pretended to give him a stern look. "But if you must know, no, I'm not planning on a toothbrush drive. Nothing wrong with treats in Christmas stockings."

"Not as long as they brush, right?"

Katie sniffed at him. "Exactly."

Will squinted and tilted his head. The way he regarded Katie made her wonder what he was thinking. She fussed with her hair before turning to the sink to wash her hands so she wouldn't have to endure his kind of torturous scrutiny. She liked having Will's undivided attention but not when she couldn't read him. He was probably thinking she was uptight, an old maid before her time. That wasn't exactly the impression she wanted to give. Katie knew the kind of girls that caught his attention—beautiful, fun-loving, carefree. She wanted him to think of her like that.

He finished his apple and tossed it in the trash, wiping his mouth with the back of his hand. "What are you really picking up?"

"I'm collecting food for a Christmas luncheon I'm putting on for people in town who might not otherwise have a place to go." Listing on her fingers, she said, "I've got most of the food donations, the plates and utensils, some of the decorations. Still looking for a place to host it, but that'll turn up."

"That's very…Katie of you."

Katie jumped as Carol pushed her way back through the door, radio in hand. "Katie of huh?"

Will's face looked tight. Had Carol interrupted when Will wanted some time alone with Katie? No. She chastised herself for entertaining such a silly thought. "She was telling me about her Christmas luncheon."

"Oh, that. Yes, she's such a darling." Carol beamed. "Can you believe she came up with that idea all on her own? So thoughtful."

Dropping her gaze, she tried to take Carol's praise gracefully, but having Will there made her feel shy about it.

"That does sound like the Katie I always knew," Will agreed. Katie pressed her lips together, unsure of whether she should smile or frown. Katie's charitable efforts either were solidifying a reputation as a dowdy do-gooder or, maybe worse, it was making her appear so angelic that she'd seem to exist outside Will's sphere of interest. Did guys like girls that were too good to be true? "You need a hand picking stuff up? I'm helping my dad today but should be done no later than seven. That's when the grain elevator at the co-op closes today."

"No, no," Katie refused, surprised by his offer. She resisted the urge to smack herself in the forehead. What was she thinking? It would have been the perfect opportunity to test the waters with Will, maybe get the ball rolling, and flirt a little more openly with him as a gateway to letting him know how she'd felt about him for so long. Maybe he'd forever be untouchable and out of her league in more ways than one, but if she didn't give it a try, she'd forever regret it. Problem was, she couldn't go back on her rebuttal now. "That's a long, hard workday for you. I can manage."

Will raised his eyebrows. "Ah. Right, I forgot. You're a strong, independent, modern woman who doesn't need anyone."

"It's not that," Katie said, laughing at Will's jab. "Your sister's already helping me. Otherwise, I would take you up on your offer. I honestly don't think I could fit another person in my car *and* all the food I'm picking up." As if on cue, Katie's phone trilled in her pocket. Pulling it out, she looked at the screen. "Speaking of, Charlotte's calling right now."

Answering the phone, Charlotte spoke before Katie could even say hello. "I'm sorry!"

"Sorry about what?" Katie asked.

"I'm not going to be able to go with you today. I've had to totally rework my schedule to accommodate the people I had to displace when Mrs. Stanley came in unexpectedly." Dropping her voice to a whisper, Charlotte said, "She forgot to set the timer for the whitening shampoo in her hair. You know, the blue kind for old ladies? While it was setting, it ended up dying her hair a very lovely but very permanent shade of blueberry. She feels awful."

Katie smiled at the thought of Delores with a halo of blue hair, but vowed never to say a word to another living soul about her blunder. It had to be mortifying to make that sort of mistake. "No worries. Honestly. I can get it myself."

"Are you sure?" Charlotte asked.

"Positive. You take care of your clients. I can get the food in my car. I am going to count this as my exercise today, between lifting frozen turkeys and cleaning out your mom's chicken coop."

"Chicken coop?"

"You know. The one at your family's house. I offered to help do some chores so they don't fall too far behind on things while your dad's recovering."

"Katie, you're going to make me look bad. You're a better daughter than I am."

Katie laughed. "I'm not trying to upstage anyone. I know you've never liked cleaning out the chicken coop. I honestly don't mind. It's kind of…therapeutic."

"You're so odd." Charlotte was silent a moment, a clear indication the cogs in her brain were turning. "Take Will with you."

Katie's heart bounced in her chest and started beating somewhere right above her collarbone. The thought of driving around with Will in her little blue coupe was thrilling, especially when she stole a glance at Will and his eyes were dancing with unspoken amusement. He had to know that Charlotte was suggesting the exact same thing he had.

"It's fine. Seriously."

Charlotte protested, "But you drive an itty-bitty car that barely has enough room for you and your purse."

"If I have to take two trips, it'll be okay. I really don't have anything else to do today. You worry about Delores and get her looking fabulous again and I can take care of the food. No worries."

"You're the most stubborn person I know," Charlotte said with a small laugh. "Have it your way. Wear yourself out in the service of others because that's what you do, but if you change your mind, you should take Will with you. It'd do him some good to have you rub off on him by doing some charity work."

Katie lowered her voice. "Didn't he just donate a several million dollars to a children's hospital?"

"Well, yeah, but writing checks is the easy part. He needs to get his hands dirty once in a while."

Katie rolled her eyes. She knew she'd never win with Charlotte unless she conceded at least a little. "We'll see."

"Good. Gotta go. I'll catch up with you later."

Katie hung up, turning back to Carol and Will. Carol was already scrubbing off the apples with amazing efficiency while Will chopped them into pieces before they went into the juicer. He worked slowly, one analyzing eye on Katie.

"What?" she asked, slipping her phone back into her pocket.

"Charlotte flake on you?" Will asked.

"It's not like that," Katie protested. "She had a legitimate emergency come up at work."

Katie moved next to Will, reaching for another knife and cutting board to help him catch up with the mound of apples Carol had already washed. She was humming along with Bing Crosby's rendition of *I'll Be Home for Christmas* and seemed to be totally oblivious as she worked.

"Someone burn their hair off with a curling iron?" Will quipped.

Katie snorted. "Not exactly, but yeah, we're talking about that level of hair emergency."

"I'm going to have to insist, then," Will said.

Tipping her head, Katie stopped chopping apples. "Insist on what?"

"Going with you."

Katie picked up her knife and sliced an apple in half. "Don't worry about it. I'm—"

Will put down his knife and ducked his head down to meet hers. "I'm more than happy to let you be independent and all, but my offer to help isn't totally innocent."

"Is that so?" Katie grinned, thinking that she'd said almost the same thing to Carol when asking about helping with the apples. Secretly, Katie had wanted more time at the Ryan's so she could sneak a peek at Will. "What are you hoping to get out of all of this?"

While he thought, Katie stole a quick look at his handsome face. How she wouldn't totally melt being around him, spending at least a couple of hours in close quarters with him, she'd never know. "I can't quite put my finger on it exactly, but I have a feeling my time with you is going to be well-spent."

CHAPTER 4

W ill jiggled his leg as he sat at the curb of Katie's small, but neatly kept, bungalow, coaching himself before he got out of the brand new, loaded, cobalt blue Chevy truck he'd bought for his parents. They'd let him borrow it for the evening so he didn't have to take his rental. It wouldn't have been able to fit many grocery donations either. He'd lost track of how long he'd been sitting there, and he still hadn't gotten out to knock on her front door. The door was the color of sunshine and was as bright as Katie's smile. It suited her.

"It's not a date. I'm only helping her get the stuff she needs for her luncheon so she doesn't have to pick it up alone," Will muttered to himself, running his fingers through his freshly washed hair. "I'm being neighborly is all. Taking care of my sister's best friend. It's not a date."

Will knew he was lying—he couldn't even look at himself in the rearview mirror. After he'd called Katie to confirm where to meet, he'd hurried to park the combine, jogged to the house for a quick shower, barely ran a comb through his hair, and used a generous helping of cologne, hoping he didn't have any residual sweat or diesel odor clinging to him. After slicing apples, he'd spent the morning trying to help his dad harvest, but when everything went wrong and they had to call it quits, the first thought that jumped into his head was that he'd get to see Katie earlier than expected. He was surprised how thrilled the thought of spending time with Katie made him.

She'd always been friendly and he knew she had a good sense of humor and an adorable laugh to match but he'd never really admitted to any sort of attraction to her. Now, something was definitely different. Being around her sent a zip of excitement through him that he hadn't experienced with any other woman he'd dated in Texas. Small town life had preserved her from the pressure of high stakes, big city dating where everyone was in a cutthroat competition to pair off. She'd stayed innocent in a good way.

Drawing in a deep breath to try and calm his pounding heart, he cracked his knuckles, then drummed his fingers on his thighs, counting down from ten. Reaching for the door handle, he was surprised by a knock on his window. Katie smirked as he jumped like a startled horse. Getting out of the truck, he rubbed the back of his neck, feeling foolish.

"I was just about to go knock on your door," he said.

Her eyes caught the light and danced with amusement. "Uh huh. You were out here for ten minutes. At least."

Will opened his mouth to protest, but he couldn't think of a valid excuse for sitting in the car so long that didn't make him sound like a creep or a coward. "You were spying on me?"

She raised a shoulder. "I was running a few minutes late. I promised my neighbor I'd watch their house while they are out of town for the weekend. I was across the street, getting their mail and watering their plants."

"And spying on me."

"Yep." Katie laughed once more and it eased the tension from the situation in an instant. "Give me a second to run and grab my purse? It's got all the addresses where we need to pick up the donations."

Will nodded, leaning against the truck as he watched her go. She ran with the obvious gait of a jogger, and she was swiftly in and out of her house, making sure her white icicle Christmas lights were on. The sunlight was a soft gold as it started to set behind the neighborhood and he couldn't help but soak her in. She'd replaced her old jeans and flannel shirt with a long scarlet sweater and leggings with a busy but stylish print. Zipping up her jacket, she tossed her sleek brunette hair behind her shoulder. As beautiful as she was cleaned up, Will had thought she was just as attractive dressed down, wearing ripped jeans with her hair piled up top in a messy bun.

She waved him over, pointing at her car. "Come on. I'll drive."

He shook his head, grinning at her. "We'll hardly be able to fit a couple of cans of corn in your trunk. I'll drive."

Katie tucked her keys back into her purse and strolled over to him with a wry smile. "This doesn't have anything to do with your need to feel macho, does it?"

Walking to the passenger door, he opened it for her. "Where would you get that idea from?"

"All those trashy tabloids you keep showing up in. They paint you as the sort of guy who likes to take control. Be in charge. An alpha male."

Will chuckled, jogging back around to his side of the truck. "I'm going to tell you right now, you shouldn't always believe what you read, especially in those magazines. And no, me wanting to drive isn't a macho move. Your car is kind of pathetic, you have to admit."

Katie tipped her head back and laughed. "What is it with

you Ryans hating on my car? I'll have you know it's a very comfortable, economical vehicle."

"It may be, but I think my knees would be in my chest if I tried to get in."

Katie giggled. Will liked being able to make her happy. "Alright. You drive, I'll navigate."

"Don't you need a map?" Will asked as he started the engine.

A slow smirk slid across her lips. "You seem to forget I've lived in Holly Wreath my entire life. I basically know this place like the back of my hand. I do, however, have a list so I don't forget anybody."

"Sounds good," Will said, slinging his arm across the back of the seat. For a second, he considered retracting it—he didn't want Katie to think he was trying to hit on her—but figured it'd look dumber if he seemed indecisive. Besides, he felt drawn to her. Her hair was a few inches from his hand and it looked so soft. It took all his willpower to focus on the road ahead of them instead of twisting a strand of her hair around his finger. "Where to?"

Katie pulled a list from the front pocket of her purse, glanced quickly over it, figured out the best route, and sent a text to the first few people who were offering donations to confirm they were home. Directing him where to go, he rolled away from the curb, not in any hurry to get where they needed to be.

Tossing her list up on the dashboard, she asked, "What brings you over here before the sunset, anyway? I thought you and your dad were working until the evening, and according to my watch," she pulled back the sleeve of her jacket and twisted her wrist toward her, "it's only four in the afternoon."

Will kept his eyes on the road. She'd asked him another tricky question that would make him sound like the worst farmer on the face of the planet if he answered honestly. "Yeah, that was the plan."

Katie delicately touched Will's arm but retracted like she'd touched a hot stove, brushing her hair behind her ear instead. "Please tell me you didn't ditch your dad to help me. I can pick all this stuff up by myself. I might be a girl, but I'm not a weakling."

"Oh, I know. I remember when you punched me."

"Punched you? When?"

"I was a junior. You were still in middle school. You slugged my arm when you came over to watch a movie."

Katie scrunched her nose. "When you stole my popcorn?"

"Barely a handful." Will kept from smiling by running his finger across his mouth. "I swear, I saw stars and had a bruise for a month."

Katie's laugh filled the truck cab. "Okay, if a little tween girl could hurt you that badly, maybe you shouldn't be touching her popcorn. You had your own bowl."

"I'd finished it and wanted more."

"Next time, you should ask."

Will swallowed. He'd like a next time. They could snuggle on the couch with an entire buffet of popcorn if that's what she wanted. He'd even let her choose the movie and endure a sappy romance if it meant he could have his arm around her shoulders while she leaned onto his chest. He had to shake his head to free himself from his fantasy. Not because he didn't enjoy it, but because he was afraid he might run a stop sign or drift off the road if he wasn't paying attention.

Shifting in her seat to face Will, Katie's eyes had taken on a look that conveyed her seriousness. "All joking aside, your dad isn't working all by himself is he?"

"No, no," Will assured, "it's nothing like that. The work came to an unexpected halt, and there's nothing to be done about it today."

"Is everything alright?"

"Yeah," Will said slowly. Rubbing the back of his neck, he admitted, "I sort of got the grain wagon and tractor stuck in a patch of mud. Neighbors won't be able to help us get it out until tomorrow morning."

Katie looked out the window, her fingers pressed against her lips. With a sideways glance, Will tried to figure out what she was thinking. Unexpectedly, a snort escaped her, followed by full-on giggling.

"What?" Will asked.

Between breaths, Katie spit out, "Your mom is right. You really are becoming a city boy."

Will shook his head, trying to suppress his own laughter but failing miserably. As he joined Katie, he had to agree. "It was a pretty rookie mistake on my part. I thought it was frozen solid, but it was a deep enough mud patch that it was still gooey under the ice. That's what I get for taking a short-cut. I guess I was in a hurry to see you."

Katie's laughter came to a screeching halt and her head whipped around to look at him. "You were excited? To see me?"

"Well, sure. I'm happy to help out my kid sister's best friend. It beats harvesting corn for hours on end."

Katie's faltering smile said it all. She looked back out the window and Will rubbed his hand down his face. He'd been too afraid to say the truth—he was excited to see her, not his sister's best friend. It was a cowardly thing to do and he had no idea why he was so protective of his heart around her. She wasn't the one to have shredded his heart into a million tiny fragments, after all.

They drove in silence for a few minutes until they reached their first destination, a two-story brick home wrapped in garland and Christmas lights. Will killed the engine and, shooting him a tight smile, Katie said, "I'll be back in just a second."

Unbuckling herself, Katie grabbed the handle and pulled, but the door refused to budge. She tried again.

"I can't seem to get my door open," she said, shoving her shoulder into it.

Will raised his eyebrows and teased, "You can't get your door open? I thought you said you weren't a weakling."

"I'm not." Katie rolled her eyes. "Do I have to crawl through the window to get out?"

"Huh," Will said. "Brand new truck. I wonder if the child lock is on or something."

He leaned over to reach the handle, getting a pleasant breath of Katie's perfume, a sweet combination of florals. The temperature in the cab of the truck rose several degrees as he worked the kink out of the door, trying to ignore that she had tried to steal a peek at him without him noticing. They were inches apart and the electricity between them was palpable.

"Voilà," he said as he managed to ease it open.

Katie clasped her hands together and batted her eyelashes melodramatically. "My hero."

Will chuckled at her goofiness and could feel the awkwardness melting away. Katie had a special way about her—the ability to make anyone feel comfortable regardless of the situation and it was something he truly admired in her. Though he'd only spent a handful of hours with her since being home, Will was reminded again and again that Katie was someone special.

Katie skipped up the steps to the front door, where she knocked, rocking from toe to heel while she waited. The door flung open and a middle-aged woman with a short bob of graying hair and glasses resting halfway down her nose beamed at Katie. The woman pulled Katie into an embrace and they talked for several minutes before the donation was handed over.

Returning to the truck, Katie tied the bag shut and reached in to put it in the back of the truck. Climbing back into her seat, she rubbed her hands together to warm up.

Will started the truck and backed out. "Get anything good?"

"The Smiths donated all the olives I think I'm going to need for the entire dinner, so yeah. It was a good haul."

"Black or green?"

Katie had a small smile on her lips. "Both."

Will pretended to gag as he idled in the street. "You might as well go ahead and throw away the green olives. They're just plain nasty."

Katie shook her head. "Says you. They're a perfect combination of bitter and tart."

"Nobody likes the taste of bitter. Even the word is depressing."

Laughing again, Katie grabbed her list. "Whatever. More for me and the rest of the world who have more refined palates."

Giving him directions to the next house, Will drove at the same leisurely speed in a loop around town. He and Katie bantered back and forth in a harmlessly flirtatious way, but Will enjoyed it immensely. It'd been a long time since he'd been able to slow down and enjoy this pace of life. Typically, he was a driven, hardworking man who didn't like to take a break for fear he was wasting time, but with Katie, he wanted to stretch every minute. That was another magical quality about her.

House after house, they filled Will's truck bed with donations from businesses and generous residents. Katie had turned on the radio, cranking up the volume until it was blaring Christmas music. When Kelly Clarkson's *Underneath the Tree* came on, she squealed and clapped her hands for one of her favorites, singing along with perfect pitch. While Katie danced in her seat, garnering a few funny looks from other drivers, Will went ahead and laughed at her free spirit while cheering her on.

"Aww," Katie said, turning off the radio, "commercial break."

"It's too bad. You put on a great show," Will said.

Katie let out a relaxed sigh and leaned her arm on the center console, accidentally brushing her hand against his. It sent a tingle straight up his arm and to his heart. "Music does that to me. In another life, I might've been a superstar pop singer. Maybe country."

"I don't doubt it," Will agreed. "Although, I'm not sure you would have ever survived leaving Holly Wreath, stardom or not."

Katie chuckled lightly. "I know I give off the impression that I'm afraid of stepping outside the boundaries of our little town, but I actually do enjoy traveling when I get the chance. I just like the idea of keeping myself rooted. Of having someplace to call home."

"Home can be anywhere you put your hat," Will said, glancing at Katie as he took a right turn.

"Yes, but my mom always said the tradeoff is you can't take all the people you love with you."

"Your mom's a smart woman. How is she, by the way?" Will asked. Waiting for her to answer, he realized the mood had changed in the blink of an eye when he caught Katie looking plaintively out the window, chewing on her thumb nail. When she didn't respond, Will tried to wet his lips, though his mouth had gone cottony dry. "Did I say something wrong?"

His question brought Katie out of the shell she'd retreated into. Though her mouth was holding a perfect smile, her eyes were glossy with unshed tears. She tried to blink them back, but they clung stubbornly to her eyelashes before one fell freely and tumbled down her cheek. She swiped it away, and her lips pulled wider.

"No." She let out a substantial sigh that seemed to make her shrink. "You didn't say anything wrong."

Will opened and shut his mouth like a fish tossed out of water as he thought of what to say. "No? Then why are you crying?"

"The question catches me off guard sometimes." As Will rolled to a stop at a red light, Katie turned her attention to a playground where a group of children were bundled up in coats and scarves while they went down slides and swung. Their mothers congregated on nearby benches, chatting with each other while they watched.

"That sounds…ominous."

"I suppose you haven't heard?"

He shook his head. "Is everything alright?"

Drawing in a deep breath, Katie said, "My mother passed away. Last year, right at the start of November."

Words escaped Will and he could feel his face going pale. As he tried to figure out what to say, Katie's laugh was the last thing he thought he'd hear.

"What's so funny?" Will's eyes shifted back and forth.

"You look a little like a cornered Peter Rabbit with Mr. McGregor's radishes," she said.

"I'm sorry," Will stumbled. "I just don't know what to say. It's kind of a shock to hear."

"Most people tell me they're sorry for my loss and that usually does the trick."

Putting his hand over hers, he murmured, "I am sorry."

She looked at their hands and her breathing seemed to hitch. He liked the feel of his hand over hers, but definitely didn't want her thinking he was trying to take advantage of the situation. He went back to gripping the steering wheel with both hands.

"Thank you," she said, bouncing back to her usual cheerful self. "I appreciate the sentiment."

"Do you mind if I ask what happened?"

"Cancer, actually. She put up a good fight but, in the end, God needed her back home with Him."

"I'm sorry."

Her eyes twinkled with humor. "You already told me that."

"I know. I really am, though. I mean, twenty-two, and both your parents are already gone? That's got to be rough."

"It is, but I feel like I'm coping pretty well. Dad died when I was so young that I don't really remember being sad about it, and I had a good eight months with Mom before she passed. By the end, she was ready to go."

"Oh. I'm sorry about that."

She playfully shoved him. "Will! Don't make this more awkward than it needs to be. Yes, there are days when the grief and pain still overwhelm me, but for the most part, I've come to terms with it. She was an amazing lady and I'm lucky that she was my mother."

Will worked his jaw, kicking himself for bringing up anything that would make her cry, even if it was unwitting on his part. Usually, when something uncomfortable came up with any of his casual relationships that led a girl to cry, he'd give her a hug and try to move on as quickly as possible. He didn't do tears very well.

Not unless the girl really mattered to him.

"Aren't you lonely?" he asked softly.

A corner of Katie's mouth twitched into a grin. "Should I ask you the same thing?"

"What do you mean? I'm lucky enough to still have all my family. Heck, I even have a great-grandma that's still in her right mind and can crack jokes with the best of them. Why would I be lonely?"

"You have family, but you don't spend a lot of time seeing them. That's sort of a tragedy, don't you think? Not to use the time you have to be with the people you love?"

Katie had gotten him there. "I guess you have a pretty good point."

"Besides. I've commandeered a lot of other people's families for my own, including yours."

Will chuckled and before he realized what he was doing, he brushed a strand of hair away from her face. He pulled back his hand, but a faint smile crossed her lips. She kept talking like he hadn't just invaded her personal space.

"That's probably why I am so smitten with Holly Wreath. Everyone here feels like my family. That'd be difficult to give up."

"Understandable."

"Since you've been probing me about my painful past, mind if I ask you a couple of questions?"

Will's heart tripped and he wondered just what she wanted to ask. He liked Katie, but he wasn't exactly ready to spill all his deep, dark secrets. He swallowed. "Sure."

"Why did you leave Holly Wreath?"

"I didn't. At least, not forever. I'm back, aren't I?"

Katie's eye roll was sassy and she groaned at his answer. "Basically, you did. I mean, right after high school, you shot out of here and hardly ever looked back. I'm pretty certain that the only time you come back is when you have a family emergency. I hate to be the one to tell you this, but it feels like you kind of abandoned us here in Holly Wreath."

"I see how it is. First, I'm embarrassing Holly Wreath as the town's billionaire flirt, but, somehow, I've also abandoned you. Which is it?"

Katie puckered her lips and lowered her brow as she

thought. "Both. I've always known you to be a very complex man."

Feeling flattered at her words, he chuckled. "I suppose I was ready to get away from a small town in the middle of nowhere, where I couldn't escape who everyone thought I wasn't growing up. I didn't like that people felt like they'd all figured me out. I wanted to be my own person, you know? Not only as my parents' kid."

"I understand that. Sometimes, it's hard for others to let us grow up and become ourselves, whoever that is. I mean, nobody's got it all figured out when they're a teenager."

"Exactly."

Pretending there was something terribly interesting about her cuticles, Katie stared at them as she nonchalantly asked, "And your leaving didn't have anything to do with a certain Megan Smart?"

Will's eyes snapped over to Katie. She slowly met his and he wasn't sure what to make of her gaze. It wasn't teasing and it certainly wasn't superior, but it was a mixture of something. Curiosity and sympathy?

"She may have had a little bit to do with it," he admitted.

Will turned his attention back to the darkening roads. The Christmas lights stood out in stark contrast to the inky black sky and it looked like every house in the entire town had gone to some measure of decorating. It certainly made the place feel quaint. They continued to mosey through the town, collecting the last of the donations, including four enormous turkeys and six honey-smoked hams before heading back to Katie's to store it.

"Now it's my turn to say I'm sorry." She ran her hand down his arm and he didn't mind the gesture in the least. "I get that not everybody is compatible, but to go and crush someone's heart the way she did is truly inexcusable."

"You know how she broke up with me?"

51

One of Katie's shoulders bounced up and back down. "Charlotte."

He grunted. He should have figured Katie would find out through his sister. "I guess I was a little naïve when it came to love, but my high school self was seeing us together long term. I'm glad it ended when it did, though. It would have been a lot more difficult if she'd drug it on for years and years."

"I bet she's regretting dumping you now."

Raising his eyebrows, he gave her a sideways glance. "Are you saying I'm a catch?"

Katie sniffed. "For what it's worth, I would never treat you like that. Or any man. Nobody deserves that kind of treatment. Especially you. Or anybody."

Was it the romance of Christmas music still playing at the back of his mind, or was Katie Holloway flustered? If he wasn't imagining things, she might have been imagining what it might be like to date Will.

The best part was Will didn't mind the insinuation one bit. He'd done his own daydreaming about Katie himself.

"I appreciate the sentiment." He made a right turn and Katie's house came into view. "If it makes you feel any better, I haven't completely given up on the idea of finding my soulmate."

"Soulmate?" Katie screwed up her face. "You believe in soulmates?"

It was Will's turn to shrug. "Well, sure. I mean, look at my parents, or the Stanleys, or the dozens of other couples that live in Holly Wreath. They're all living testaments to the idea that love can be enduring. You just have to find it."

"Then why all the serial dating in Austin? You have a new girl with you every time you get your photo taken."

Will backed expertly into Katie's driveway and put the truck in park. "A lot of them are friends, the rest of them have been fun. I figure there's no harm in having a good time while I look."

"As long as no one's getting their hopes up and getting hurt, right?"

Katie's gaze was questioning and he felt pressure to answer tactfully. "Sometimes, heartbreak is the casualty of the dating experience, but yes, I do try to make sure no one thinks I'm too serious before I do anything that would resemble commitment."

Watching him briefly, Katie seemed satisfied. "Good. Now I'd better get your truck unloaded before everything melts."

"Let me help get it unloaded." He looked over his shoulder at his truck bed, which was easily halfway full of groceries, disposable plates, and plastic cutlery. "There's absolutely no way you could have fit all this into your itty bitty car. Not even Santa and his elves could have pulled off that kind of magic."

Katie stuck her tongue out at him, eliciting a laugh from Will. "Go ahead and rub it in, that my car is more suitable for clowns in a circus, but I'll be the bigger person, and thank you for your help. I couldn't have done it without you. Well, I could have, but it would have taken me all night." Leaning over, she quickly brushed a soft kiss on his cheek. "Thanks."

She shifted in her seat, her face concealed by the darkness as she struggled to open her door again, leaving Will to analyze her kiss. It was brief and chaste, but it would have been enough to knock him on his butt if he weren't already sitting. He kept his hand from touching the place where her lips had barely grazed his cheek, but there was real power in such a simple act. It took all his self-control not to wrap his arms around her waist, scoot her close, and press his lips firmly on her mouth.

Katie tried fruitlessly to let herself out, eventually letting out an exasperated sigh. "I don't think this truck wants me to leave."

Will thought how he didn't want her to leave either, but he caught himself before he said it aloud. Will reached across her and wiggled the door open, feeling Katie's eyes on him the whole time. As the door swung open, she jumped out and met him at the tailgate.

Clapping her hands, she vigorously rubbed them together. "Alright. Want to race to see who's the fastest? Or should we see who can carry the most overall?"

"Are you always this competitive?"

"My mom always said if a little friendly competition gets the job done faster and makes it more fun, I should always be ready for a challenge."

"I wish I would have known your mom better."

Katie's smile widened. "Don't worry. She would have loved you as much as I do."

Wondering if he'd heard her right, he didn't have time to dwell on it because Katie was already halfway up the driveway with a tray of canned pumpkin puree.

"Hey!" he shouted, grabbing a frozen turkey in either hand. "That's cheating."

"Did I not say go? Ready, set, go!"

Will ran to catch up, but as he dumped the turkeys in her deep freeze, she'd already run back and was carrying the bag of olives, stacking them with incredible efficiency on an empty section of shelves. They were slowed by uncontrollable laughter, and Will's fingers were nearly numb by the time he finished carrying all of the frozen foods, but he didn't care. He couldn't remember the last time he'd laughed so hard that his stomach ached, or had so much fun doing anything that resembled work. He especially enjoyed the flirty smiles and glances that Katie would give him as they passed on the driveway. They made his heart rate kick it up a notch.

"Done," Katie said with satisfaction as she tossed the final packages of cranberries into the freezer.

She was panting slightly, but Will had to lean over to catch his breath. "I've always been garbage over long distances."

Katie snorted. "Long distance? Hardly. We maybe ran a mile with all those passes up and down the driveway." He stood up and she poked him square in the abs, teasing, "I think you need to talk to your personal trainer and get on some cardio routines instead of only weights."

He'd already tossed his leather jacket onto the grass in the middle of emptying groceries, and had been running in his t-shirt since he'd dropped off a load of ice cream. Striking a pose, he flexed his muscles, making Katie laugh and, if he wasn't seeing things in the dim light of her garage light, blush at his antics. "Are you saying you don't like the results?"

"No. But if you don't like being beat by a girl whose legs are a good six inches shorter than yours, you might want to jump on the treadmill once in a while."

"Oh, ho, ho." Will laughed. "I see how it is. You name the time and place and I'll be there. In fact, want to race right now? We could run to the corner and back and see who's gloating after that."

Before Katie could answer, her stomach rumbled so loudly she gripped her midsection, trying to hush the noise. Her already pink cheeks turned a shade of red. "Apparently I have an ogre living in my stomach, and it's angry."

"You're hungry?" Will asked. He wasn't an idiot. If he hadn't been able to recognize a good opportunity when it arose, he wouldn't have been able to build a social media empire as quickly and efficiently as he had.

"Well, yeah! Aren't you? I mean, I've been thinking about

Christmas dinner and what all I'm going to cook the entire time we've been lugging the food to my garage."

Will grinned. "Me, too. Wanna get a bite to eat?"

Katie's smile disappeared off her face. "Oh, no. You've already done enough today. I don't want to tie up your entire evening. I bet your mom has a yummy, home-cooked meal waiting for you."

"Katie," Will said, putting a hand on his hip and shaking his finger at her in playful scolding, "you helped my mom can I don't know how many pints of apple jelly, after rescuing me from having to clean out the chicken coop. Taking you to dinner is the least I could do to say thank you."

"But you helped me pick up all the donations," Katie said, sticking her chin out in pretend defiance. "That makes us even."

"Uh, no. That's two chores for one. Where I'm from, that's not an even trade."

"We're from the same place."

"So then you should know it, too." Putting his hands on her shoulders, he turned her toward the truck and opened the door for her.

"Fine. If I have to." She couldn't even hold back a giggle as she pretended to be put out. "Where to?"

"Not the diner," Will answered. "How about tacos?"

"Now you're talking." Katie beamed at him. "It's a date then."

CHAPTER 5

A kiss on the cheek?

It's a date then?

Katie was mortified that she was being so forward. Sure, her teenage self would be in awe of her boldness, but in this moment, she was terrified. Yes, he'd offered dinner, but did she have to go calling a meal with Will more than what it was? Katie would've told anyone who asked that he was a friend—her very hot, best-friend's-older-brother friend—but in reality, they teetered on the edge of being mere acquaintances. In school, they'd run in different circles, with Charlotte being the common denominator, and once he'd left for college, it wasn't like he'd ever called to say hello. Then, he was back in Holly Wreath for all of a week, and Katie kept jumping at the chance to spend time with him. She was all about being up front with guys she dated, but there were always some clear expectations from both sides. As ambiguous and uncertain as Will and she were, her behavior was bordering on desperate.

"Nice night," she said if only to break the silence that permeated the cab. "I'm surprised we haven't gotten more than a dusting of snow yet. It almost doesn't feel like we're only a couple of weeks from winter without a proper snow."

"Oh, it's on its way. I hear there's snow in the forecast. I'm hoping we can finish harvesting before we have to shovel snow out of the cornrows so we can get the tractor through."

"After you get it out of the mud, of course."

Katie winced, hoping she wasn't crossing a line, teasing him too much. A wave of relief hit her when she caught sight of his grin. "Right. Mud first."

"You'll get it done. You might have to pick the corn cobs off by hand, but you'll get it done."

A rumbling laugh came from Will. "As long as you come help."

"Looking for free labor?"

"Looking for good company."

Katie thought about reaching over to touch his hand, but maneuvered instead to scratch a phantom itch on her cheek, then tucked her hands under her legs so she wouldn't make that pass again. She'd been openly dalliancing with him all afternoon and, though it'd been exhilarating, she knew she was treading into dangerous territory. She would risk her heart if she wasn't careful. Moving too fast might lead to the sort of heartache she wasn't ready to endure. It would be another goodbye, on the heels of letting her mother go, that she wasn't sure she could recover from.

Will drove slowly through Holly Wreath's main street. "The Tex Mex Oasis still as good as I remember?"

"Are you crazy?" Katie looked sideways at him with a smirk. "They've added a plate-o'-tacos that's so good it should be outlawed."

"Careful. You're getting my hopes up."

The way he looked at her with a hunger in his eyes made her wonder if there was a double meaning to his words.

In an effort to protect herself until she could have time to sort out the feelings that were hitting her from every side, she infused humor back into the situation. She jabbed him in the arm, enjoying the firmness of his bicep beneath his clothes.

"Oh, quit," Katie said. "You know as well as I do that Tex Mex Oasis doesn't mess around with their food. You're going to seriously consider moving back to Holly Wreath by the time we're done with dinner."

"Maybe I won't care about moving back. I've been known to do rash things after a good meal."

Katie sniggered as they pulled into the parking lot.

Will circled the entire building, searching for a spot. "Looks like they're busy."

"Do you want to try somewhere else? I'm not set on tacos."

"You can't do that to a man, Katie," Will said.

"Do what...?"

"Promise him all the tacos his heart desires, only to take them away from him before he's even had a bite. That's a level of cruelty no woman has ever been brazen enough to inflict upon me."

Laughing, Katie agreed. "That would be unfair of me, depriving you of Mexican food, especially after all the help you've been."

Finding a space at the back, Will pulled in and put it in park. "Besides, I'm not in any rush. Are you?"

Catching her lip between her teeth, Katie shook her head. "I'm not. Other than a thirsty philodendron at home, no one is expecting me. Besides, I imagine most of the other restaurants are probably packed, too."

"A philo-what?"

Katie twirled the end of her hair and chuckled, realizing how lame she'd just made herself sound. "A philodendron.

It's a house plant. The only thing I have at home that would care if I went missing is a house plant."

"Well, I'm sure that philodendron loves you very much."

Will slid out of the truck, and instead of leaning over to open her malfunctioning door, he walked around the back to her side. With a second alone, Katie quickly checked her hair and makeup in the mirror. She fixed a feral loose strand that wasn't lying quite right and slipped on a coat of lip gloss before Will opened the door and offered his hand to help her down. She accepted, coyly placing her fingers in his, relishing the rippling tingles that zipped through her body. When he let go, her hand felt cold, and she acutely missed holding his hand.

Will stuffed his hands in the pockets of his jeans to ward off the biting chill in the air since the sun had set. A few flurries drifted lazily from the sky, making the restaurant look warmer and inviting. "It is Friday night, I guess. Date night for a lot of customers."

Katie's heart unexpectedly jumped in her chest. Maybe she hadn't been too bold in calling dinner a date, if he was willing to call it that, maybe things were headed in the right direction. A slow, steady step. She could roll the anxiety out of her shoulders caused by the fact that she was falling for him at reckless speeds.

Will held open the door for her and they wove their way through people crowded in the waiting area. The inviting, balmy, spicy aroma of Mexican food enveloped them. Katie gave their name to the hostess and they stepped aside, waiting their turn to be seated. Taking in a deep breath, Will let out a satisfied sigh.

"Ah, yes. This place will do."

A waitress scooted out of the kitchen with a tray full of chips and salsa and Katie involuntarily began to drool, kind of like the way she did the first time she laid eyes on Will at the diner. In a word, he was yummy. "Good. Because I don't think I can leave without at least getting a basket of those chips."

"Hey! Katie!"

Katie and Will both turned toward a familiar voice. Charlotte was heading their way. Excusing herself as she hurried through the crowd mingling right inside the door, Charlotte towed Harvey behind her. Katie recognized Harvey from the dentist's office. He was the kind of patient who never had a cavity and was always prompt and polite. She liked him and his mellow personality seemed to suit Charlotte the way black and white complimented each other. Katie's eyes flashed to their intertwined fingers, then up to her friend's face. Charlotte winked as an unspoken answer. Apparently, things with Harvey were going better than Katie had suspected. She made a mental note to grill her friend about it when she had a chance to get Charlotte alone. If Katie managed to work up the courage, she might even confess to her friend that she had a thing for her brother. In her head, it was still an uncomfortable conversation with Charlotte, but better a best friend than a complete stranger fall for him, right?

"What are you two doing here?" Charlotte asked, snuggling up close to Harvey.

Charlotte was a tall girl, but Harvey had several inches on her, so when he let go of her hand and reached across her shoulders, he could easily accommodate her under the crook of his arm. He'd barely spoken a handful of words to Katie personally, beyond what was required to check in for a dental cleaning, but Katie could tell he was full of personality behind his bashful nature. His handsome face had most definitely sealed the deal, too. Judging by the elated smile glued on his face, he was more than a smidgen head over heels with Charlotte, too.

Will snorted. "It's obvious, isn't it? We're going to stuff ourselves with Mexican food."

Katie poked her thumb at Will and corrected, "*He's* going to stuff himself with Mexican food. I'm going to eat a moderate, sensible amount because, unlike him, I can come back to the Tex Mex Oasis whenever I want."

"Texas has good Mexican food too, you know," Will mentioned.

Katie folded her arms and smugly answered, "The Tex Mex Oasis would beat any restaurant you put it up against, hands down."

Will's hazel eyes flashed over to Katie's. "It's going to take more than food to convince me to move back. Or not. You keep claiming the tacos are that good."

There was that delicious look in his eyes again.

"You're so ridiculous." Katie scoffed. "So back and forth about what motivates you. I can hardly stand it."

"If you can't stand it, feel free to sit down."

Holding in a laugh as long as she could, Katie eventually gave up and burst out giggling. "That was a horrible pun."

Will folded his arms across his chest and asked, "Then why are you laughing?"

"Because it was so awful!"

Laughter continued to flow, and though she knew she probably looked like a fool, the amusement on Will's face was enough to keep it going. Charlotte looked equally entertained, though Katie didn't miss that there was a question in her eye she knew she was going to have to answer later.

Both of them were going to have some answering to do.

Sobering herself, Katie apologized. "Sorry. I've always loved a corny pun and that one caught me off guard."

Charlotte gave Katie a look. "I'm not sure you should be laughing. It'll encourage Will's lame jokes even more. Are you sure you didn't catch too many fumes when you were cleaning the chicken coop, or is there something else going on here?"

Charlotte bounced her eyebrows suggestively, and immediately, the air was sucked straight out of Katie's lungs. Her mind raced as she tried to come up with a plausible answer, but nothing seemed adequate. At least not without Katie totally spilling her secret and confessing that she'd had the hots for Will for a desperately long time.

Cool and collected, Will answered for the both of them. "Goodnight, Charlotte."

The hostess came to show Will and Katie to their seat, and Katie thanked her lucky stars for the hostess' timing. They left Charlotte grinning like the Cheshire cat, with Harvey's arm still draped across her shoulders. The redheaded hostess guided them through the busy restaurant to a booth toward the back. Several people seemed to recognize Will and whispered behind their hands about him striding past, but Will continued to move through the restaurant, unfazed by their gawking. He had to be used to his celebrity status by now. There probably wasn't a warmblooded woman within a hundred mile radius that wasn't drawn to his magnetism, which meant he was probably pretty good at dealing with all sorts of attention.

An ounce of self-doubt seeped into Katie's thoughts, making her wonder if she was a total fool for even admitting to herself that she *wanted* to be with Will. He could have any woman he laid his eyes on. What was so special about Katie?

"Katie," Will said, grabbing her wrist and pulling her into his chest.

The move surprised her, and her heart leapt into her throat while a flurry quickened in her gut. Looking up into Will's hazel eyes, she was sure there was longing there. Though their friendship was still in its infancy, to say nothing of a relationship, Katie's imagination ran wild. Was he going to kiss her? Right in the middle of the restaurant for everyone to see? Their lips were certainly closer than they'd ever been.

Tilting her chin up to him to make sure her lips were available, she breathlessly asked, "Yes?"

Will's eyes moved to something behind her, and she looked over her shoulder, following his gaze. A waiter straining under the weight of a tray full of sizzling food hurried past. Putting two and two together, the fluttering butterflies in Katie's stomach crumbled and died. He wasn't trying to kiss her—he was rescuing her from crashing into the waiter.

"Didn't think you wanted to be wearing chips and salsa," Will said.

Katie's smile drooped—she'd been hopelessly daydreaming that Will had been thinking about kissing her and it wasn't even a plausible possibility. What had she been thinking? He certainly had pulled her in close enough that the scent of his spicy aftershave was intoxicating and she swore she could smell cinnamon gum on his breath. Recovering quickly, she stepped back, flicking her hair behind her shoulder. "That's what I'd get for not paying attention. Thanks for saving me from myself."

"Sorry about that," the hostess said, scowling at the waiter as he hurried to his table. "Sometimes the waitstaff are so tunnel visioned when they come out of the kitchen."

"Can't keep the customers waiting," Katie said, cringing at her own forced cheerfulness. Without looking at him, she asserted, "Thanks for...intervening, Will."

"What else am I good for if not hauling tons of canned food and saving damsels in distress from runaway tacos?"

Katie chuckled, wondering if he could hear her heartbeat, which was still pounding in her own ears. Even if she hadn't gotten a kiss from him, she could still enjoy the feel of being in his arms. It felt sort of like being home.

The hostess motioned them forward with a flick of her fingers, and Will placed his hand on Katie's lower back, gently guiding her to their booth. Spotting a few old high school friends, Katie waved, trying to appear as natural as possible to anyone who might be watching. As she sat down, she took the menu from the hostess and stopped the urge to fan her burning cheeks by staring at the words.

"Well, I already know what I want," Will said, putting his menu down. "I wasn't kidding when I said I could eat an entire plate of tacos."

"You definitely worked up an appetite," Katie said, looking over her menu then back to Will. "I think I'll have—"

Right over Will's shoulder, she caught sight of someone she could have happily gone the rest of her life without seeing again. Of all the things she loved about small town living, what she loved best was that so many people knew each other. One downside was that there was no escaping the ones she'd rather avoid.

"You alright?" Will said, his brow furrowing and his eyes focused on her with great concern. He laid his hand over the top of hers and she wanted to lace her fingers between his but she couldn't move. "You look like you've seen a ghost."

Katie eventually regained control of herself. With a shaky hand, Katie took a sip of her ice water. Putting up her menu and ducking down behind it, she answered, "I wish I was seeing ghosts, but unfortunately, it's a former date."

One side of Will's mouth hitched up in a lopsided grin that made all of Katie's insides flip. He was going to tease her about it, but not until he got a good look at the guy. Putting his arm on the back of the booth, Will casually glanced behind him to see who was haunting Katie.

"The guy with the green baseball cap on?" he asked.

"Don't look!" Katie hissed. "If we're lucky, he'll leave, and I can live one more day without having to talk to him."

Scooting further down into her seat, she held her menu in front of her face, still staring at the words but not comprehending them. Holding her breath, she could feel the tension building up in her neck, forming into a tight knot in her shoulders that was going to require a serious massage to get rid of.

"Is that my Katie?" she heard over her menu.

Blowing out the stale air she'd been holding in her lungs, Katie gave herself a mental pep talk. Laying the menu on the table, Katie pasted a cheery smile onto her face. "Rex? Hi! How are you?"

"Fantastic." A toothpick balanced precariously between his lips. She didn't miss that his murky brown eyes took in more than just her face and she was grateful to have the table and her menu to hide behind. "How nice to see you."

She suppressed a shudder that threatened to rack her insides and smoothed it over with a lie. "Good to see you, too."

"Hi," Will interrupted, his hand extended. "I'm afraid we haven't met. I'm Will Ryan."

It was only when Will spoke that Rex seemed to realize Katie was sitting with anyone. Sizing him up, Rex clapped his hand into Will's and clenched. A wicked glint passed over Will's eyes and he gripped tighter.

When Rex couldn't take it any longer, he yanked his hand away. "Easy, buddy. I don't need a broken hand."

Hiding her smile behind her water as she took another sip, Katie muttered, "Those are farmer's hands for you."

"I'm not a farmer," Will countered, winking playfully at Katie. It was enough to make her guffaw dumbly while her heart skipped a beat.

"Ryan? Will Ryan?" Rex snapped. "As in Ryan Family Farms? The billionaire CEO of that new social media site?"

"Yeah," Will confirmed, draping his long arms across the back of the booth. There was a wariness as he watched Rex, like Will was ready to outmaneuver him if needed and Katie didn't doubt he could run circles around Rex, mentally or otherwise.

Rex's eyes darkened, and a vulpine smile crossed his face. "Heard your folks are having a hard time getting their corn brought in this season. That's a real shame."

Will shrugged off Rex's jab. "Happens to the best of 'em."

Katie added, "That's why he's in town."

"Ah," Rex said. "That's right. You don't live here anymore."

"I'm based in Austin, Texas, currently." Will reached for a chip and scooped up a healthy serving of salsa, fitting the entire thing in his mouth. If he was at all ruffled by Rex's attempts to ferret out any of Will's weaknesses, he didn't show it.

"That explains it," Rex said.

Katie was quickly growing tired of Rex's games—the same ones he played during their very brief dating stint. He was manipulative, arrogant, and not nearly as witty as he thought he was. Cocking her head to the side, Katie narrowed her eyes at Rex. "Explains what?"

"Explains why the rumor is running around town that you're going to the Holly Wreath Christmas Social all by your lonesome self," Rex answered, resting his fists on the table and leaning toward Katie.

A dull throb started at Katie's temples, and she massaged at it with her fingers, audibly sighing. She mumbled through clenched teeth, "Word sure gets around fast."

"That's a small town for you," Rex said with an unconcerned shrug. "Don't worry, though. I've got a solution for you."

Dropping her hands, Katie asked with the kind of incredulousness that made her words clipped, "And what is that?"

Holding his hands out, Rex proudly proclaimed, "I'm your knight in shining armor, baby."

Katie heard what he'd said, but it took a moment for her brain to catch up. Her jaw unhinged and she stuttered, "Excuse me?"

"I'm going to take you. I promise, I'll show you a real good time." Katie did not like the way he wriggled his eyebrows at her.

Before Katie could figure how to dig herself out of the mortifying situation she found herself in, Will answered. "Sorry to disappoint, but you've heard wrong. Katie isn't going by herself."

"Oh?" Rex said as he took off his ball cap and scratched at his thinning buzz cut. "And who exactly is going with her?"

Will looked over at Katie, and he placed his hand over hers.

"Me."

CHAPTER 6

Will couldn't believe his dumb luck. He'd been trying to find a way to bring up the Holly Wreath Christmas Social in a way that would open up a conversation about the possibility of them going together when Katie's ex sashayed in and made it all too easy. In fact, it had gone better than he could've imagined. If there was one thing he'd learned, it was that comparison against other guys always made Will win out in the end and he wasn't afraid to use that fact to his advantage when the situation warranted it.

While Rex stuttered, trying to figure out how to weasel his way into being Katie's date instead, Katie secured Will's plan by lacing her fingers through his.

Katie smiled kindly but confidently at her ex. "Sorry, Rex, but I'm afraid Will is right. As you can see, I *do* have a date for the social."

If the night could have gone any more perfectly, Will didn't know how. He'd all but forgotten about the tractor getting stuck in the mud and that the setbacks on his parents' farm meant he would have to stay longer than anticipated in

Holly Wreath, a thought that no longer irked him like it had when he'd first come back. He may have left the town in a huff, ready to escape the disappointment Megan Smart had caused him, but Katie was quickly replacing any bitter memories with experiences that were much sweeter.

They ate until they couldn't take another bite, talking until they were the last ones in the restaurant. The best part was there was no question that Katie was flirting with him. She'd accidentally brush her toe against his leg while she crossed one leg over the other, or would meet his gaze demurely, watching him under her dark lashes. He'd done his fair share, too, making sure to hold her hand as much as possible.

Riding home in the truck, he purposefully took a few wrong turns so he could spend a few more moments with Katie, however he could get them. He was going to pay for it the next morning when he'd have to work all day to get the tractor out and hurry to get as much corn in as they could before he fell asleep at the wheel. Sunday wouldn't be a day for sleeping in, either. His mom would undoubtedly prod him awake bright and early so they could make it to church on time.

And, still, facing that reality, every stolen moment with Katie was absolutely worth it.

He'd put up the center console in the truck and Katie sat close enough that it made his heart hammer against his ribs, and his left leg bounced up and down excitedly. The source energizing him was that when she scooted into the truck, she'd picked up his hand and hadn't let go. Will couldn't get enough of how her fingers felt so right, intertwined with his own, like there'd never been a time they weren't together.

"Here we are again," Will said, putting the truck in park. "Hope I'm not getting you home too late."

Katie shrugged as she ran her thumb across his knuckles.

"I'm not the one who has to get up early to drag a tractor out of the mud. Maybe I'll sleep in until noon and eat ice cream for breakfast."

"Flavor?"

"Chocolate chip cookie dough."

He put on his most charming smile, the one he knew made women go weak in the knees for him. "Careful or I might be tempted to join you."

"I always have plenty of ice cream on hand. I'll consider it celebrating the fact that I now have the most handsome date in all of Holly Wreath to the Christmas social. That definitely deserves a helping of ice cream."

Scratching at the stubble growing on his cheek, Will dropped his gaze before looking back up to Katie. "About that. I hope I wasn't being too pushy."

Katie shook her head and scoffed. "Pushy? No. That's the definition of Rex. He bulldozes over everyone until they give in, hoping it'll placate him enough until he loses interest."

"Well, maybe you did really want to go by yourself. Then I went and inserted myself as your date."

Katie put her fingers on his mouth to silence him. "You honestly think I'd rather go by myself than with you? I was mostly telling Charlotte that I'd go, even if it was by myself, so she'd get off my back. I honestly figured I'd show up, make sure she saw me once, then slip out the back door and go home. I don't think with Harvey at her side, she'll see much of anyone else anyway."

"That's probably true," Will said, chuckling at his sister, who never did anything half-heartedly.

"Plus, the timing was perfect. I don't know how I would've gotten out of it with Rex. He thinks very highly of himself, and it would've taken some convincing to get him to understand *why* I didn't want to go with him."

Will's mouth twitched as he tried to keep a straight face.

"I'm having a hard time understanding how you and Rex ended up as a couple in the first place."

Katie's face turned pink, making the small, pinprick freckles on her face more conspicuous. With a heaving sigh, she rolled her eyes. "It's a long story. Basically, it was a blind date—a favor I was doing for a friend—and he sort of tricked me into a second date. As far as Rex was concerned, two dates meant we were a couple, and when I stopped answering his calls...I've been having to dodge him whenever I see him around Holly Wreath. It's a bit of a headache, really."

"I don't want to drive a wedge between you and your friend, but I think she might've been trying to dump Rex on you to get away from him," Will joked.

Laughing, Katie agreed. "I'm positive that's what happened, which would explain why she always looks so guilty when she sees me. I can't blame her, though. The dating pool gets smaller and smaller every year. I'm barely into my twenties, and already feel like I'm going to die an old maid."

"Maybe the right guy hasn't come along yet."

Katie smiled bashfully. "Maybe I was needing to wait for the right guy to come back."

Katie's words were direct and poignant. In her dark eyes, he could see a glimmer, hinting that she had been wanting him longer than he realized. How he'd missed it was beyond him, but in the faint light of her Christmas lights, that revelation made him feel emboldened. He was ready to make his move, never mind that it might be forward to kiss on their first date. It was time he had a happy memory in Holly Wreath when it came to a girl. He had a feeling it'd be a perfectly blissful memory for Katie as well.

Will took both of Katie's hands and edged his way closer to her until they were thigh to thigh. He draped his arm across her shoulders and she reciprocated by looping her arm around his waist. Will would have been happy staying right there, searching her eyes, studying her lips.

Her eyes flicked down to his mouth and back up, while her own lips curled into a cute but slightly diabolical grin. "I bet you're a great kisser."

"Yeah? You think so?"

"I've always kind of assumed you were. I mean, how could a guy who's so good at everything he puts his mind to *not* be good at it?"

"I'm not sure if I should kiss you or not then."

Katie's eyebrows dropped low and her smile slipped down into a slight frown. "And why's that?"

"Maybe it's better to leave it all to the imagination. I'd hate to disappoint."

Her smile returned. "I doubt you've ever disappointed anybody."

He leaned in closer and stopped right before his lips skimmed across hers, pausing significantly for effect. "Shall I give you a taste?"

"Yes, please. That would be a Christmas wish come true."

Drawing Katie in, he gradually closed the gap until his lips met hers. The kiss was slow and sweet but was entirely austere.

"Katie?"

"Hmm?" Her eyelids fluttered open.

"I'm going to need a willing participant if I'm going to give you a proper kiss." He stroked her hair away from her face. "You don't need to hold anything back."

The way she nibbled her lower lip made Will want to kiss her all over again and never come up for air. She moved her chin up a notch and he pressed his lips against hers once more. The electricity between them was amplified as she let down her guard. The kiss was brim-full of passion and pent-up longing, speaking volumes between them without a word. Like holding her hand, it felt so natural to be kissing Katie Holloway.

After what felt like an eternity that was somehow magically wrapped up in an instant, Katie pulled back, while he kissed along her jawline. She sighed happily, a faint chuckle coming up her throat, and she touched her forehead to his. Will's resolve to stay away from Holly Wreath came crumbling down. Any more kisses like that with Katie and he'd return to his hometown without ever looking back.

"That was...amazing," Katie murmured. "Hands down, best kiss I've ever had."

"I was thinking the same thing."

"You're not just saying that? You've probably had a lot more experience than I have."

He knew Katie's opinion of him had been colored by how the media outlets had portrayed him, but her question offended him enough that it hurt. He might seem like a billionaire player, but he hadn't gone around kissing every girl who threw herself at him.

"No. I mean what I say." Will kissed the back of her hand. "I'm a man of my word."

"I believe you."

"When will I see you again?"

Katie leaned over for one more soulful kiss that sent another shock of adrenaline coursing through every last inch of Will. Pulling away, she touched his cheek.

"Soon."

"Not soon enough."

"How about I bring you and your dad some lunch tomorrow afternoon?"

"I'd like that. Think we can sneak in another kiss, too?"

"After tonight, I'm thinking anything can happen."

She leaned back so Will could help open her door. It was

hard watching her go. He couldn't remember the last time he'd fallen so hard for someone that it ached being apart from them. Trotting up to the front porch, Katie twiddled her fingers and blew a kiss as she disappeared inside.

Will inhaled deeply, grinning foolishly to himself as he pulled out of the driveway and headed back to his parents' house. His heart thudded in his chest, reliving the entire evening over and over, especially how fantastically it had ended.

The Christmas lights were still on when he pulled into his parents' driveway, and he bounded up the steps. Quietly opening the back door, he tiptoed so he wouldn't wake his parents. It was already past midnight and they were never ones to be night owls. Will filled a glass of water before he headed up to bed to try and sleep. The morning was going to come sooner than he'd want it to, and if he didn't get some decent sleep, he'd be paying for it later. Whether asleep or awake, he knew he was going to be dreaming of Katie. With a pleasant buzz of happiness still running through his veins, he started whistling a sporadic, happy tune.

"Have a good evening?"

The question startled Will, and he spun around, clutching his hand to his heart and barely keeping the glass he was holding from slipping out of his fingers.

"Dad? What are you doing up? You about gave me a heart attack."

Roger looked over the silver rims of his bifocals and smirked. Grabbing a cookie from the Oreo bag, he dunked it into his milk. "I've been sitting at the table the whole time. If I wanted to sneak up on you, I guarantee you would've had that heart attack."

Will chuckled and wiped up the water he'd sloshed onto the floor with a paper towel, then pulled out the chair next to his father and took a cookie. Copying his father, he poured himself a glass of milk, held down the Oreo until the bubbles stopped, then popped it in his mouth.

"What are you doing up so late?" Will asked, taking another cookie.

"I was wondering the same thing," Roger said, leaning back in his chair and locking his fingers behind his head. "Hot date?"

"How did you...?" Will trailed off as he tried to solve his own question. It came to him as he replayed the evening. "Charlotte."

Roger belly laughed. "You know she can't sit on a good bit of gossip when she has it."

"She's become the stereotypical hairdresser," Will said, pinching the bridge of his nose. "I imagine her running into Katie and me tonight will be the highlight of the hair salon."

"For a month. At least," Roger said with a one-sided grin.

"Dad," Will said with a groan, "don't say it like that."

His dad belted out a laugh but smothered it into his hand. Hitching his thumb toward the staircase, Will pointed out, "You're going to wake up Mom, and I guarantee she's not going to be happy knowing you're eating Oreos at midnight."

Roger batted his hand at his son's comment. "What makes you think she doesn't know I do this? I couldn't keep a secret from your mother if I tried."

"Then...why?"

Will's dad shrugged. "You having a date with Katie Holloway of all people is a pretty big deal. So? How was it?"

"It was...good."

"Good?" Roger asked incredulously. "Just good?"

"Dad," Will said flatly, "it's weird that you're so invested in my dating life."

Roger laughed softly as he took out one last cookie, then closed the package. "Actually, your mother and I are more concerned about Katie."

A dry smile crossed Will's lips at his father's confession. "You're worried about Katie?"

"Son, I don't know what your plans are for the future, and, of course, we wish you the best in all your endeavors, but to say we'd love to have you back in Holly Wreath is an understatement. Part of us feels incomplete that you flew the coop and made your home so far away. When it comes to Katie, though, we don't want to see her with a broken heart. She's already had enough of that in her short life. Plus, she's out of your league."

Roger nudged Will playfully, and both of them laughed. "No arguments there," Will agreed.

"Seriously, son. Katie is someone special. Don't go and mess that up."

Staring out the large kitchen window above the sink, Will could see the clear night sky and pinpricks of stars hanging in the dark expanse. There was no mistaking Katie was one of a kind. A faint shooting star dashed across the sky and on an impulse, he let himself make his own Christmas wish. All he wanted was to have a chance to explore the possibility of Katie for as long as they both needed, even if that meant forever.

"I know she's unique," Will said. "I promise I'll do my best not to screw up with her."

"Alright, son. That's all we ask of you."

Excusing himself to go to bed, Will went up the creaky wooden stairs as quietly as possible so he wouldn't wake his mother. That was, if she wasn't already wide awake from his dad and him conversing and laughing in the kitchen.

He didn't know how long he laid awake in bed, but sleep had been elusive as he tried to unsnarl his thoughts. The next morning, Will woke with the sunrise, the beams of sunlight streaming in through the gossamer curtains. Putting his arms behind his head, he pulled a deep breath into his lungs and exhaled. He felt like he'd barely gotten in twenty minutes of rest, but as he relived the night before—holding Katie's hand and that fantastic series of kisses they'd shared, he didn't care.

Hearing a firm knock on the door, his father's voice drifted through the solid oak. "Ready, Will?"

Will sat up and twisted his spine and reluctantly let go of his reverie. "I'm awake."

"Daylight's burning, and *someone* got my tractor stuck in the mud, and we have to get it out before we can finish up the corn."

Slipping a tattered old t-shirt over his head, Will laughed. "Be down in a minute."

His stomach rumbled, ready for the full breakfast his mother was cooking downstairs. As he inhaled the heavenly, savory aroma of bacon and eggs that floated up to his room, he hurried to check stock prices, answer a couple of urgent emails, and reassured the company board that he hadn't fallen off the face of the earth.

In the middle of skimming a newspaper article, his phone rang. *Charlotte.* He hesitated answering. He'd already had a talking to from his dad and he didn't particularly want one from his sister. He knew better than most that Katie was someone special. It'd been made obvious the more time he spent with her. She was unlike any other woman he'd known. She was cute in an adorable kind of way, but was mature and wise beyond her years because her circumstances had demanded it. He couldn't get enough of her laugh and he could stare into her eyes for as long as he drew breath. He knew things were changing so fast. Normally, it might have scared him, but Katie was an anchor to him. Holly Wreath was no longer a bane, and Katie had muddled his resolve to leave as quickly as possible.

His phone stopped ringing, but before he could let out a

sigh of relief, Charlotte called right back.

He scrubbed a hand down his unshaven face and answered. "Hi, Charlotte."

"Did you just wake up?"

He didn't answer right away. "Is that why you're calling? To see if I'm up early on Saturday? Because if I remember, you know how to drive a tractor, too. Maybe you ought to be out here helping."

"I would, but in case you forgot, I have a business here."

"The old ladies couldn't wait for a haircut?"

He could almost hear Charlotte pinch her lips on the other end of the phone. "I'm going to pretend you didn't say that."

"What are you calling for then, if not to be teased by your older brother?" Thinking back to last night, he smacked his hand against his thigh. "Wait a minute. Is this about Katie? 'Cause I already had a heart to heart with dad last night about our date because of you."

"I thought you said it wasn't a date."

He smirked. "By the end of the night, it very much was a date."

"It's not about Katie."

"What is it then?"

Charlotte drew in a long breath and Will ground his teeth together, annoyed by her dramatics. "You haven't heard?"

"Obviously not."

"Oh. Maybe I shouldn't mention it then. The situation might pass without it even affecting you."

"Charlotte!" Will snapped. "Either tell me or don't, but I don't have time for this. Spit it out."

"She's back."

Will racked his brain, trying to figure out who on earth 'she' might be. He drew a blank. "She, who?"

"Megan," Charlotte said. "Megan Smart is back in town."

CHAPTER 7

A s much as Katie wanted to spend every waking moment with Will, she barely got half an hour with him when she went to deliver a picnic lunch of sandwiches, sliced fruits and veggies, and chocolate chip cookies the size of Will's hands as a treat. She'd met Will and his father, Roger, in the field and, though it was only noon, both of them looked in dire need of a nap. They parked their tractor towing the grain wagon and the combine mid-row and hopped out, slogging slowly to where Katie had pulled over on the gravel road.

When Will was close enough that she could see the details of his face, she could see his smile was genuine, but it didn't fill his entire face. Something was off. She tried to keep her mind from galloping away with worst case scenarios, but she had a propensity for doing just that. She'd had plenty of experience with it after all—her mother's cancer diagnosis had been every bit as terrible as she feared it would be, leaving her parentless before she'd even really stepped foot into adulthood. Taking a calming breath, she focused on the here and now, and seeing Will made her happy. His less-than-all-in smile probably had to do with the fact that he was running on barely any sleep and still had a good twelve hours of work ahead of them. She knew they'd work until midnight, when Roger would call off the harvest at midnight so they could rest on Sunday.

It didn't help things that there was no way to sneak away and steal a kiss. Will didn't even give her a hug since his father was the third wheel to their meal.

She didn't let the disappointment settle. Things were going to be different on Sunday and she was going to see to it. The Ryans hadn't missed a Sunday church service in as long as Katie could remember and they took their day of rest seriously. That meant Will was going to have the entire day off, even if they hadn't finished bringing in all of their corn. After church, he might go home and have lunch with his family and take a nap, but the rest of the day she was going to greedily insist he spend with her.

The following morning, Katie danced in her bathroom, humming along to the Christmas playlist she had on her phone while she finished unrolling the curlers she'd put in her hair. She'd learned a few tricks from Charlotte to putting soft waves in her hair, but mostly, the body she could create came from her mother's hair. When her mom had freshly washed hair, it would curl ever so slightly into enviable waves that only a handful of people seemed to effortlessly have, thanks to good genetics. Seeing her hair do the same thing as her mother's, with a little help from the curlers and styling products, Katie smiled at her reflection as she remembered her mother, feeling closer to her as Katie's brunette hair made her look like her mother when she was younger and before she was sick.

Checking her phone, Katie squealed. "Shoot!"

She'd tried on half a dozen dresses, trying to find the one that would hug her curves in all the right places, but wouldn't make her look like she was trying too hard. She was going to be at church after all. As she'd rifled through her closet, she'd totally lost track of time and even if she left that instant and sped all the way to the modest white chapel for church services, she was going to at least be five minutes late.

Slipping on a dark navy blue belted dress, she matched it with a pair of cute leather boots. They were sensible but they gave her a bit of height that would bring her ever so slightly closer to Will's lips, should he want to kiss her again. Then, she wouldn't have to stand on her tiptoes. She grabbed her gray pea coat and a cold bagel for breakfast, holding it in her mouth as she ran everything out to her car.

As luck would have hit, she caught every single red light on the way to church. She knew it was in consequence of her own vanity. She vowed to do better next week to get to church on time, but still, she smirked to herself. She was going to knock Will's socks off with her outfit. A little tardiness would be worth it.

Katie arrived eight minutes late and had to squeeze her car into a spot next to a minivan that had parked on the line. Her door barely opened, but she flattened herself against her car, hoping she wasn't wiping the dirt from her car off on her dress. Doing a quick once-over when she'd made it out of the tight spot, she dashed to the entrance of the church. The opening hymn, sung by the choir, filtered outside, inviting Katie in. She stealthily snuck in, making sure the door closed without a noise behind her. Finding a pew at the back, she gave a few smiles at people who turned to give her curious looks. She managed to turn their disapproving frowns into understanding smiles.

Sitting up straight in her seat, she craned her neck to see if she could spot Will. She didn't have to look very long—a pair of gorgeous hazel eyes was looking right back at her.

She twiddled her fingers and he waved discreetly back

until his mother nudged him and reminded him to pay attention. They were in the front row after all and people would notice if he was looking around instead of listening.

As hard as she tried, Katie couldn't seem to pay attention to the preacher. The choir was beautiful and the message—what little she heard of it—was stirring and motivated her to be better. But, as much as she relished her contemplative hour every week, she was ready for church services to be over. She was craving a quiet moment alone with Will and, if she didn't get it soon, she might chew all her nails off as she channeled her excitement.

When the prayer concluded with an amen, Katie was out of her pew in an instant. She lost sight of Will in the congregation, as people began shaking hands in greeting and filtering toward the side room where the smell of hot coffee and fresh donuts fragranced the air.

"Katie! Katie!" A girl with freckles across her cheeks not unlike her own and a radiant smile came running over to her.

"Hi, Heather." Katie put her hand on her head, messing her hair playfully. "I think you've been growing on me again. Are you taller than the last time I saw you?"

Heather's mom, Olivia, walked up behind her. "It sure seems like it. She can put away a couple helpings worth of dinner and still ask for a snack twenty minutes later."

Heather shrugged. "I can't help it. I'm growing."

"Well, don't be in such a hurry to shoot up." Katie gave her a one-armed hug. "I still remember you when you were a baby."

Katie and Olivia caught up, chattering about work in the dental office, or how business had been at Olivia's bed and breakfast. Olivia was a single mom and worked harder than anyone Katie knew, but somehow, she managed to always look unruffled. Katie was going to have to ask for her secret someday. Like the sermon, Katie tried to keep her focus on the conversation at hand, but her thoughts kept wandering over to Will. She was eager to see him. He was wearing his Sunday best, and that included a dark charcoal gray suit that accentuated the width of his sturdy shoulders. She'd seen photos of him online in one of his custom-made suits, but she was sure it was something entirely different to behold in person.

Heather stepped away and narrowed her eyes, appraising Katie. "I like your dress. It's a nice color on you."

Katie held out her skirt. "You think so?"

"Yeah," Heather said. "Are you trying to impress someone?"

Olivia's mouth nearly dropped to the floor. "Heather!"

Katie fought a losing battle over a blush that was creeping up her neck. She grinned at Heather's cleverness. "Maybe."

"Is it Mr. and Mrs. Ryan's son?" Heather asked.

Olivia's eyes shifted from her daughter to Katie. She was just as curious as her daughter, but was polite enough not to prod.

"When did you become so clever?" Katie asked, chuckling as she brushed her hair behind her shoulder.

Heather shrugged. "I notice things, especially when I get bored in church. He kept turning around and making eyes at you."

"Okay, that's enough." Olivia put her hands on Heather's shoulders and started guiding her toward the refreshments. "I think we're going to get a donut before going home."

Katie waved goodbye to them, smoothing her hands down the front of her dress, hoping her trembling hands would calm themselves. If she didn't find Will soon, she was afraid her nerves would make her explode into a million pieces. Since when had she become so lovesick?

It wasn't every day that her lifelong crush noticed her in a way that made her go limp in the knees.

His goodnight kiss a couple nights ago definitely had something to do with it, too.

Skirting around a group of older couples who were having a lively conversation about their grandchildren, she looked for the front pew where Will had been sitting. Her insides dropped when she couldn't see him anywhere.

"Looking for someone?"

A hand around her waist made her squeal loudly enough that a hush replaced the murmur of conversation and dozens of pairs of eyes turned toward them. Giving the preacher a penitent smile, she let Will guide her outside, where they could be away from prying eyes.

"Will," she slapped at his chest after she put her coat back on, "I can't believe you. The preacher's going to call me in for a meeting if you aren't careful."

Will whispered in her ear and his hot breath tickled her neck, making a heavenly shudder roll up and down her spine. "Then we'll have to be careful."

He bent down and his lips were so close to hers, when someone spotted them and interrupted at the most inconvenient moment.

"Will?" A woman's sultry voice practically purred his name. "Is that you?"

Feeling Will's spine stiffen under her hands, her own chest tightened, making it harder to breathe.

Competition.

She should have known that was highly likely with Will. Katie was only hoping that she'd get more time with Will to secure his affections before they were put to the test.

Will's hands dropped from Katie's sides and he spun around. "Megan. How nice to see you."

Leaning around Will's shoulders to see if it was *the*

Megan, her heart froze solid and sunk. The dark hair tumbling past her shoulders, cool, blue eyes, the magnificent figure. Yep. It was Megan Smart in the flesh, matured by a few years of absence which only made her look more incredible.

As if offering a cruel joke by Mother Nature, snow started tumbling from the low-hanging clouds. Instead of feeling magical, it felt like a representation of Katie's insides—cold, lifeless, bleak.

Megan sauntered over to Will in heels so high Katie wouldn't even dare put them on, her eyes fixed on him like he was the last piece of chocolate cake on the platter. Katie's mouth went dry. With each step Megan took toward them, Katie shrunk under her shadow. Megan had always been larger than life, especially when Katie was so close she could literally see that Megan was flawless. In an instant, Katie was reduced to being a timid freshman watching a confident, gorgeous senior Megan, who'd never so much as glanced at Katie and had always had Will wrapped around her finger.

"Will," Megan said in a breathy voice as she pulled him into a hug. "It's so nice to see you."

Looking like a deer caught in the headlights, Will wasn't trapped there long. He recovered quickly with a dashing smile that had probably gotten him out of all sorts of sticky situations. He hadn't become as successful as he had by letting anything catch him unaware.

He put his arms around Megan in a hug that lasted entirely too long for Katie's liking. Swallowing her jealousy, Katie plastered a smile on her face, but unsure of what to do with the rest of her. She shifted from one foot to the other, stuck her hands in her pockets and jiggled her keys, let her eyes wander from Will to Megan and back again.

"What are you doing in town?" Megan brushed a fuzz off of Will's suit.

Katie lost her resolve, watching Megan put her hands on Will. If she couldn't smile, at least she could keep her face neutral. It had to be better than scowling. She was not one to be the jealous type but Will brought it out in her. Now that she finally had him, Katie wasn't about to let him go without a fight.

Will smoothed a hand down his tie. "I'm helping my parents get things done around the farm."

Megan arched an eyebrow in question. "Thinking of picking up farming again?"

"Nah." Will laughed softly. "My dad hurt his arm and he's so stubborn, he wouldn't hire out anyone to help, so he got pretty far behind."

"Oh, no." Megan put her hand on Will's arm and it took all of Katie's willpower not to audibly scoff and roll her eyes. "Is he alright?"

"Yeah. He's on the mend and, if things go well, we should be all wrapped up before the end of next week."

As the silent observer, Katie's mind flashed to the inevitable. Will was going to finish working for his dad, and even if he promised to take her to the social, there was a big, gaping hole in their future after that. He had made his home in Austin the same way Katie had made her home in Holly Wreath. They might as well have been living lightyears apart.

"I'm glad to hear that." Megan's smile was dazzling and she seemed to mean what she said. "It's so hard to watch parents age. I always kind of thought mine were invincible until recently."

"Is that what brings you to town?" Will's attention was on Megan the way a hawk focused on the prey it circled over-head, but when his hand searched for Katie's and he gripped it tightly, her heart soared above the clouds. It was a small gesture that let Katie know she wasn't an afterthought in his mind. "Last I heard, you'd moved out to California."

Megan expertly tossed her hair and renewed her smile. "That's right. My parents moved out there too so they could enjoy the warmer weather. We're actually back to have an early Christmas with my sister and her kids."

"Nice," Will said. Looking down at Katie, she met his eyes and felt her insides melt a little bit. "You remember Katie, don't you?"

Megan squinted at Katie, trying to jog her memory. "You're Charlotte's friend, right?"

Katie nodded, unable to find her voice.

"How's Charlotte, by the way?" And just like that, Megan had grazed over Katie and was back to batting her eyelashes at Will.

Katie kept her laughter to herself. Back to being invisible to Megan. Will adjusted his grip on Katie's hand and when he did, Katie couldn't care less what his former girlfriend thought.

Will and Megan caught up while Katie listened silently. It wasn't nearly as uncomfortable being privy to their reunion when Will kept feeding her little hints of his affection. A glance here and there, a smile just for her. Will might have been being polite but his mind was clearly on Katie.

"Megan! We're going to the car!" an older woman with silver hair and the same blue eyes as Megan called from the church steps. "Meet us there?"

"Okay, Mom!" Megan smiled, turning back to Will. "I should probably go. I don't think my family is going to appreciate that lunch is late because I was yakking with you."

"It was nice to see you," Will said. "Hope you enjoy your visit."

"I always do." Megan's eyes moved to Katie. "Nice to see you again too, Katie. I love your dress, by the way."

Katie was shell-shocked by the compliment and could barely manage to eke out a word. "Thanks."

Walking a few steps away, with her hips unnecessarily swaying for Katie's liking, Megan spun back around. "How long are you in town for, Will?"

He shrugged. It was a question Katie had been wanting to ask him for a while. "At least through the end of the week. Then I'm going to play it by ear."

"You know what?" Megan walked back to him and pulled one of her business cards out of her coat pocket, holding it between two fingers and offering it to him. Katie chastised herself for not being more assertive. Surely Megan could see that Will was already taken. Or maybe he wasn't. A couple of hours, dinner, and a passionate kiss weren't enough to assure that they were exclusively dating, was it? "We should catch up over lunch sometime. It would be nice to hear what you've been doing the last few years. Why don't you give me a call when you're available?"

CHAPTER 8

Will should have torn Megan's business card in half the second she was out of sight but he'd slipped it into his coat pocket, and there it remained like a brick, weighing heavily on his mind.

He wasn't interested in Megan anymore. She'd made it clear when they'd broken up that she'd moved on to greener pastures with the high school quarterback. Tom? Travis? It didn't matter what his name was. He was pursuing Katie and was happy with his choice.

Still, curiosity got the best of him. Part of what had been so difficult for him when Megan severed their relationship was that he hadn't gotten the closure he'd needed. Now, the chance had presented itself, and he decided to take it.

He'd sent Megan a brief text on Tuesday night, after he'd gone to dinner with Katie. They'd talked about nothing in particular, enjoyed good food and a break from the constant work of the farm, and as the evening drew to a close, they shared a few kisses that had left him wanting more. It solidified his resolve that Katie was the kind of woman he'd needed all along. He'd tried the career-driven, loud, attention-seeking women who always seemed to run in packs in big cities, but they'd never totally impressed him. Katie was the antithesis of them all, and even though she was sweet to her core and constantly put others before herself, she had a wicked sense of humor and knew how to have a good time. He was falling hard for Katie and he didn't care one bit that it was derailing his plans.

Will opened the door to the only Italian restaurant in town and stomped the snow off his shoes. Ever since Sunday, they'd had on again, off again snowstorms that had severely slowed the harvest. He and his dad were only getting a few dozen acres done a day, if that. With a forecast full of snow on Wednesday, he had asked his dad if he minded that he run to town for lunch since they weren't going to get out into the field.

"Meeting with Katie for a bite?" Roger asked as he heated up for himself an enormous mug of hot chocolate for breakfast.

A twinge of guilt hit him in the gut. "No. Just business."

"Well, if I were you, I'd drop off some flowers at Katie's office to let her know you're thinking of her. Women like those kinds of spontaneous shows of affection."

"I'll remember that," Will said, dumping his breakfast dishes in the sink and heading upstairs to shower.

He almost turned around three times on his drive to the restaurant, but he didn't like backing out on his commitments, even if he regretted making them in the first place. Scanning the lobby of the restaurant, the guilt was so heavy he nearly crumpled under the burden and headed back to his truck. About to leave, Megan looked up from her phone and her entire face lit up.

"Will!" she waved and stood up, trotting over to him.

Giving him a quick peck on the cheek, he couldn't bring himself to mirror her smile. What would Katie think of their meeting? He hadn't mentioned it to her. It would have only made her worry. She hadn't said anything about Megan, but it was clear as day that she was uncomfortable with the thought of his ex being in town. He would have a quick meal with Megan, tell her he had gotten over her, wish her all the best, and finally be able to put her in the past where she belonged.

Megan draped her red coat over her arm. "I already put our name on the list. It shouldn't be too much longer." She tilted her head to one of the benches, which had a wreath hung above it. "Come. Sit down. I feel like it's been forever since we've seen each other."

Before they could sit, the hostess called their names and led them to a booth with a window overlooking main street. Megan took one side and glancing out the window through the snow shower, Will gulped. He hadn't realized as he drove in how close the restaurant was to the dentist's office. Kitty corner and across the street. It wasn't likely, but Katie might spot them. Maybe he should have been smarter about his choice of restaurants.

Maybe he should have been smarter and not come at all.

Megan tugged on his sleeve and giggled. "Earth to Will. Are you going to sit down?"

"Oh. Right." He took off his coat and hung it on the hook at the end of the booth. "Sorry. Lots on my mind."

Megan rested her chin on top of her fists. "Good thing I'm still an excellent listener."

Sliding into the booth, Will pulled out the menu and decided on his order. Megan kept quiet, watching him with her intense and perceptive eyes, waiting for him to be ready to talk. They ordered, talked briefly about the weather, but otherwise sat in silence. The waiter, wearing a black apron and expertly carrying their tray of food without breaking a sweat, set down a helping of linguini and chicken in front of

Megan, and cheese stuffed ravioli with a side salad for Will. They ate a few moments in silence, when Megan wiped her mouth with her napkin, and set it in her lap.

"You weren't kidding when you said you had a lot on your mind," she said.

Laughing to himself, he scratched at his left sideburn. "How could you tell?"

"You always clam up when you've got a lot to say, like you're trying to dam it all up instead of let it out, then when it comes out, you drown everyone in the vicinity with your thoughts."

"Yeah. Bad habits die hard."

"So, then let's start slow. Tell me, how are things going with you?"

"Good. Running a business has been fulfilling. I'm really proud of everything I've built and am excited to see what the future holds for me and my employees. Social media is always evolving, but when it comes down to it, it's all about connecting people."

"Alright." Megan steepled her fingers together and nodded. "Thanks for the live TV interview response. Now tell me how you're really doing."

Will poked at his noodles with his fork. "It is good, but running a business, maybe especially a global one, has its own challenges. Sometimes, it gives me such a headache I can barely see straight, you know?"

"I do." Megan nodded.

"I saw on your card you're in real estate."

"Yep. Just started up my own company recently, too. I like being my own boss, but until I find a reliable personal assistant, that means I have to do *everything* myself. This is the first vacation I've had in almost two years."

"That's tough, but I'm proud of you. I remember how you were always going on home tours with your mom for fun when you saw a house that was for sale. Now I bet you get your fill."

"Yeah, I am living the dream in a lot of ways."

"Not in everything?"

Megan shrugged. "Is that even possible? I think it's natural for people to always be wanting something more. I haven't put my finger on what that is yet, though."

Will nodded. "I get it. Nothing wrong with having life goals and striving for something."

"Right. Yeah."

Megan took a drink of her water and pulled a breadstick apart, letting the conversation ebb. Will tried to eat, but his appetite hadn't ever really showed up. He kept peering across the street, wondering what Katie was up to. He did have a bouquet on the front seat of his truck for her, just like his dad had suggested, that he was planning on delivering after lunch, and since he'd arrived to meet with Megan, all he wanted to do was leave and cross the street to Katie's workplace.

Megan reached across the table and put her hand on his. Her fingers were soft and slightly cold, but it surprised Will how familiar her touch still felt over eight years after their breakup. "Okay. This is awkward. You're holding back and I don't think you need to. Now spill."

Her intuitiveness caught him off guard and he did his best to keep his expression neutral, so she couldn't read him like an open book like she used to. As friendly as she was behaving and as much as she had matured, Megan still was the girl who had ripped his heart to shreds all those years ago.

He wiped his mouth and tossed his napkin on the table. "I've been doing some thinking since being back in Holly Wreath."

"About?"

Will shrugged lamely. "Life. Where I'm headed. If it's the path I want to be on."

An amused smirk crossed Megan's pretty face. "A billionaire CEO before you're even out of your twenties and you're wondering if you're on the right path?"

Chuckling as he ran a hand through his hair, he dropped his eyes to his lap. "It sounds ridiculous when I say it out loud, doesn't it?"

"Not really. I was giving you a hard time, that's all." Megan sat back against the booth and folded her arms, dissecting him with her gaze. "There's more to life than career success, isn't there?"

A weight lifted off his shoulders. He was surprised Megan seemed to understand his dilemma in a way most people couldn't. He had everything most people wanted, but there was a space that was empty. Incomplete. "Exactly."

"Does this maybe have to do with that pretty little lady that was on your arm at church on Sunday?"

Without thinking, Will's eyes went back to the dentist office across the street. He had no doubt that Katie had been in charge of the decorations in the office. A single electric candle was in every front facing window and a wreath so big he could jump through was hung over the front door. The office seemed unassuming, yet charming and familiar. Sort of like Katie.

He blew out a breath. "Yeah. This has a lot to do with her."

"Tell me about her."

Will's shoulder's wouldn't stop shrugging. "How do I sum up an entire person, especially one who I've barely been spending any time with until this week? It's ludicrous that she means so much to me so quickly. I mean, I'm not the kind of guy to fall so hard, so fast."

Megan took a sip of her water and looked out at the snow, hypnotized as it fell. "I think that kind of answers my question. She's cute. And no, she doesn't seem like your usual type."

"Maybe that's what's so appealing. I've been looking in all the wrong places this whole time when she was right under my nose. I should have been paying closer attention."

Megan tossed her hair behind her shoulders and leaned back over the table, drawing him in with her eyes. "I'd like to think I kept you happy, if only for a time."

"We had a lot of fun together."

They ran into another wall of silence and to keep from staring into Megan's dazzling eyes, he did a quick sweep of the restaurant. The lunch rush was ending, leaving them in an increasingly empty building together. He had the sudden resurgent urge to toss a hundred on the table, tell the waiter to keep the change, and run across the street to surprise Katie with the mixed flowers he'd stopped by the florist to buy.

"Thanks for letting me get that off my chest," Will said softly. "I haven't told anyone any of that yet. It's been... helpful to say it out loud."

Will started gathering his things when Megan's hand shot out and landed on his arm. "Hang on there. My request to meet wasn't totally benign either."

He froze. "What do you mean?"

Megan pressed her rouged lips together, smoothing out her lipstick. "Will, there's something I need to say before I chicken out."

Using his food as an excuse to remove his hand, he twirled the noodles onto his fork. "Go for it."

Megan took a deep breath and Will could tell her heart was hammering in her chest. Her nervousness put him on edge, too. "For a long time, I've wanted to apologize to you. For how I hurt you in high school. It was an immature, selfish thing of me to do. I wish I could say I was trying to figure myself out, or something more poignant, but honestly, it was simply a matter of letting my devotion slip. I thought I could find greater happiness elsewhere and it turns out, I was wrong."

A pair of crystalline tears rolled down Megan's cheeks and crashed onto the white tablecloth where they soaked in.

Will never liked seeing Megan cry. Feeling the need to do something about it, he pat her hand in a platonic show of comfort. "Hey, it's in the past. I forgave you a long time ago and I don't think you should be beating yourself up over mistakes we both made as kids. It's part of growing up."

Megan took a shuddering breath and composed herself, delicately dabbing her napkin along her cheeks to keep her makeup intact. "I appreciate that. Thank you for being the bigger person and realizing that people can improve. At least, I like to think I have."

"You have. Some guy is going to be lucky when he catches your eye."

Megan smiled at him, but her chin wobbled. "That's kind of part of the problem."

"Problem?"

Lowering her voice so Will had to lean in to hear, Megan confessed, "I still don't think I'm over you."

CHAPTER 9

"What am I going to do?" Katie asked, feeling her lungs constrict, unable to draw a deep enough breath to clear the panicked feeling that was edging its way into her body.

"First of all, calm down. Sit." Charlotte put her hands on Katie's shoulders and pushed Katie down into her salon chair.

Katie obeyed, thankful that her friend had let her come in last minute. Charlotte usually kept her shop closed on Thursdays but when Katie had called after work, asking if she had a minute to talk, she'd told Katie to meet her over at her salon. The space was chic and trendy, decorated a lot like Charlotte's house, and Katie felt completely at home there. She'd had a lot of great conversations with Charlotte while she trimmed the ends of her hair, always keeping it right above her shoulder blades. Charlotte had turned on the music to some upbeat, contemporary Christmas music that, for the most part, was a touch too modern for Katie's taste, but sounded enough like Christmas that she couldn't help but hum along.

"Something's not right," Katie muttered as her thumb nail found its way into her mouth and she started to chew.

Charlotte nudged her hand away. "No nibbling."

"I can't help it. I can tell something's the matter."

Taking out a brush, Charlotte began running it through Katie's hair. "Okay, start from the beginning."

"You were there at the beginning."

Looking at Charlotte's reflection, Katie watched her scrunch her face. "Are you talking about at the diner?"

Katie shrunk into her chair a little deeper. "Before that."

Charlotte stopped brushing. "What? Are we talking kindergarten or something?"

Laughing, Katie shook her head. "I was aware of him when I was in kindergarten, but I don't think I realized I had a crush on him until later. He was always cute, though."

Charlotte pretended to fake gag. "Okay, stop. I realize you have feelings for my brother, and I'm glad you finally came and told me about it, because I wholeheartedly approve of you and him as a couple. I mean, who better to fall in love with him than my best friend? But fair warning, if you start talking about how cute his butt is, or how he's a good kisser, I may throw up. Remember, I'm related to him."

Another hearty laugh escaped Katie and it flushed the nervousness right out of her. Charlotte knew how to put things into perspective and could do it with humor.

"Alright," Katie said. "I apologize for telling you I think your brother is hot."

Charlotte made a face at her in the mirror. "So, you've got the hots for my brother. What's got you on edge, then? Things seem to be going really well for the two of you."

"As often as I get to see him it's been amazing, but he's been really busy helping your dad."

"Yeah, but that'll be over soon enough. That's kind of how a farmer's life is. Busy during some seasons, then the rest of the time, they can sit around and watch the corn grow because they don't have anything else to do."

"But Will's not a farmer."

The words seemed to choke Katie, and her throat closed in on itself.

"Ah," Charlotte said. "You're worried that once he's done with helping our dad, he's going to be back out the door and on his way to Texas without a second thought for you."

"Basically, yeah."

"Okay, first of all, stop being so dramatic."

Katie barked out a laugh. "Me? The dramatic one? I think between the two of us, you're infinitely more emotional."

"Which is why I can recognize it so readily in you. It's not like you to be uptight about…anything."

"So I'm not allowed to worry?"

"It's not that. What I'm saying is I don't think you need to be worrying. Have you seen Will lately? He's been walking around like a lovesick puppy dog. He's totally wrapped around your finger."

"It started out so well. When he walked back into the diner with you, I decided it was life giving me a second chance and I was going to take it."

"Then why were you so resistant to me suggesting he take you to the Christmas social?"

"For one, I didn't want to have a pity date, especially from Will. That would make me feel pathetic. For another, I wanted to pursue him on my own terms. I didn't want him to look at me like all I am is his little sister's friend. I wanted him to see me for who I am."

Charlotte nodded. "I can respect that."

"Then, when you called and canceled on me to help pick up the donations and Will stepped in to help, it felt so natural to be spending time with him. We knew enough about each other that we could talk without that awkward, getting-to-know-you phase. I already know what makes him laugh, he already knows I like to help other people."

"He didn't know about your mom, though." Charlotte pulled several pairs of scissors out of her drawer and set them on her tray. "I should have probably filled him in on that so he didn't stick his foot in his mouth like a dufus. Sorry."

"It's fine. I don't expect him to know everything about me. I mean, that's part of the fun of dating, isn't it? Discovering something new about the person you're invested in?"

Charlotte got a dreamy, faraway look in her eye. "Yeah. I guess that's true, though whenever Harvey and I have a chance to talk, we end up making out. Maybe I should take your advice and talk to him a little more or all I'm going to know is that he's a great kisser."

"So's Will."

Charlotte shoved her fingers into her ears. "*La la la.* I can't hear you! Will's my brother, remember?"

Katie covered her eyes with her hand apologetically. "Sorry! It slipped out."

"I'll forgive you. This time."

"Thanks." Katie's leg started jiggling in the chair and the anxiety she'd been feeling about Will's behavior returned full force. "Still, something seems like it's off."

Charlotte shook her head. "Excuse me? After all this wonderful stuff you've had to say, coupled with my testimony that Will's never been this happy, you're still sure something is wrong? You're not going to be one of those clingy, whiny girlfriends are you? 'Cause I can tell you right now, that act rarely goes over well for anyone."

Charlotte motioned Katie to the wash station, sat her down, and reclined her head into the sink, running a stream of hot water down her scalp that massaged her skin. Katie involuntarily shuddered and felt every muscle fiber relax.

"I'm not trying to. I mean, I saw him Saturday and just figured he was tired. Then Sunday, we ran into Megan after church."

Charlotte froze. "He talked with Megan?"

"Out in the parking lot, after services. She saw him and ran over to give him a hug and he gave her a hug back. I'm kind of surprised she didn't go ahead and kiss him right in front of me."

"A hug? How long are we talking? Like a friendly, two-second hug, or something longer?"

Katie ran her hand down her face. "Does it matter? I didn't want her hands on him at all. Would you be okay with watching Harvey hug one of his exes?"

"No, and that's a fair point, but you have to understand that's the kind of a precarious position Will's life puts him in."

"What? He has to hug every gorgeous woman that comes running his way?"

Charlotte squeezed a dollop of shampoo into her palm and rubbed it into Katie's hair. "No, not exactly. But his job does entail a lot of public relations. He has to keep people happy to make sure his company does well."

"We're not talking about his job though. We're talking about personal relationships. Shouldn't he be okay with offending his ex for the sake of keeping the girl he's dating happy?" Katie closed her eyes and grimaced. "Maybe we aren't even really dating at all. I don't know what the rules of etiquette are for how many dates it takes for people to be exclusive. I'm so out of the loop."

Charlotte squirted the water at Katie's face to get her out of her funk. "Quit second-guessing yourself. Will likes you. Don't you worry about Megan. She's ancient history."

"She gave him her business card and said she wanted to catch up with him."

"And did he agree?"

The silence was heavy as Charlotte waited for an answer. Katie knew she was being ridiculous. "Well, no…"

"Then he's not interested. He was probably just being polite."

Katie caught a whiff of the conditioner Charlotte was working into her hair, making a mental note to take some home with her. "You're probably right."

"Of course I'm right. I'm not too close to the situation to see it for what it is."

"He did surprise me with flowers Wednesday afternoon at work."

"Well, there you go. My brother isn't completely hopeless." Sitting Katie up, Charlotte towel dried her hair and pointed back to her salon chair. Katie flopped back down, watching Charlotte comb out her hair. "What are we doing with your hair today? Are we going for a boring old trim or are you going to let me jazz up your look for once?"

"Go for it."

Charlotte stopped mid-stroke. "Excuse me?"

"I said go for it. Buzz my head and shave a smiley face into it if you think it would give me an edge over Megan."

Laying her hands on her shoulders, Charlotte gave Katie a little shake. "Hey. I'm going to tell you right now that you don't need to do anything to be on par with Megan."

"Thanks," Katie said as her eyes blurred with those pesky tears. "I think I'm letting my high school insecurities get the best of me."

"I would have to agree. But seriously, if you're ready for me to take your look to the next level, I have been dreaming of this day for as long as I've had my license."

Katie chuckled. "I do think it's time. Although promise me you won't buzz any character designs into my head. I said that in a moment of duress."

"Promise. Though you can't ask me any questions or complain about anything until I'm all done."

"Deal."

"Are you ready for this? It's going to take me a couple hours."

"I don't have anything else planned. Will is working late again with your dad tonight. They're supposed to be finishing up the last of the work today."

"Good. Then the next time you see him, it'll be a surprise."

Charlotte had the uncanny ability to chatter while working. It was impressive how fast she could go, nimbly working her fingers around the tiniest sections of hair. Within the hour, Katie's head was covered with strips of foil and while they waited for the hair color to work its magic, Charlotte pulled her over to the manicure table, chiding her for biting her nails. As a compromise to fake nails, Katie agreed to gel nail polish in a soft pink that glittered in the light.

After rinsing her hair again, Charlotte trimmed off several inches and added layers, assuring Katie it would give her hair the kind of volume other women dreamed of. Biting her tongue, Katie let her work. She had agreed to let Charlotte do her thing. Right as Charlotte turned off her hair dryer, the doorbell to the front entrance dinged.

Katie tried to look but couldn't around Charlotte's tight grip on her hair and Charlotte was concentrating too much to be bothered to glance. "Sorry but my salon's closed."

"Oh. Sorry. I'll come back later."

Katie knew that voice. Both she and Charlotte jerked their heads in the direction of the waiting area. Megan looked dressed to kill in a black t-shirt, ankle-length cable knit sweater, and a pair of leggings that proved she was every bit as fit as she'd been in high school. She adjusted her purse on her shoulder and she retreated back a step.

"Megan!" Charlotte was just as surprised as Katie felt. "Wow! How nice to see you. Come in."

"Are you sure? I really don't mind coming back later. I was doing a little Christmas shopping and saw your light was still on. I didn't even bother to look and read the hours on your window."

"My fault. I could have locked the door but it slipped my mind," Charlotte said, graciously motioning her in. "Come, sit down. What are you needing tonight?"

"Just a trim. If I don't keep on top of my hair, I get split ends like nobody's business."

"I hear that," Charlotte said. "Give me a minute to finish up with Katie and I'll get you taken care of."

Megan's eyes went to Katie's face, and Katie wished Charlotte was a little further along with her makeover. Her hair was still wild and fluffy in an unflattering way.

"Hello, Katie," Megan said. "Nice to see you again."

All of Katie's worries came crashing back down. How could she possibly compete with a woman like Megan? "You, too."

Thankfully, Charlotte took the reins of the conversation. "I heard you were back in town."

Megan chuckled. "A good hairstylist is always one of the first to know."

Charlotte made sure Katie's hair was even on both sides. "What brings you back to Holly Wreath?"

"I'm here with my folks and we're staying with one of my sisters. It's been a while since I've seen them and thought it would be fun to visit where I grew up."

"That'll be a nice way to pass the holiday."

Megan nodded, and her eyes glanced over to Katie again, though Katie did her best not to notice. "I saw your brother's back in town, too."

"He is. I'm sure you heard about my silly dad, going and

falling off the ladder. Why he didn't hire out some of these jobs or at the very least, rent a lift instead of crawling up a ladder is beyond me."

"I'm glad he'll be alright." Megan wet her lips with a flick of her tongue and sat back in her chair, crossing her long legs and looking very much like she was Holly Wreath royalty. She had won Prom Queen her senior year, so in a way, it was true. "How long is Will going to be here? Is he planning on staying through Christmas or does he have to go back before then?"

"That's the million dollar question," Charlotte answered. "He hasn't really said. He'll at least be staying through the weekend. There's the tree lighting, then the parade and social on Saturday."

"I forgot they do that. It sounds like it's a good time," Megan said.

"Have you ever gone?" Charlotte asked. "To the social? Or did you move away before you were eligible?"

"I snuck in once with one of my friends. We were eighteen and I guess technically adults, but it would have been more fun with people I knew. I can definitely see the appeal of it now."

"You should come." Katie held back a groan and wanted to ask Charlotte what she was thinking. Yes, Will had asked her to go with him, but Katie didn't particularly want Megan showing up, undoubtedly dazzling in evening wear. "I'm going with Harvey."

"Harvey Feinberg?" Megan sat up in her chair. "That cute guy who's six-foot-something and has the most tempting chocolate eyes?"

Charlotte beamed. "That's the one."

"Lucky you. My cousin said they went on a couple dates and while he's quiet, he's an absolute gentleman." Megan got some lip gloss out of her purse and smoothed it on. Who was she trying to impress? "What about you, Katie? Do you have a hot date for the social?"

While Charlotte ran the flat iron over Katie's hair to tame it, Katie looked at Megan, making sure she met her gaze. "As a matter of fact, I do. I'm going with Will."

Megan settled back into her chair, unflinching at Katie's response, but something in Megan's eyes told Katie she should watch out. It was a hunger that made it clear Megan was up for a challenge.

Or maybe she was just imagining it.

Megan was so hard to read.

"Well," Megan said coolly, "sounds like you're a lucky lady, too."

Trying to swallow, it felt like Katie's mouth was packed with sand. "Yes, I am."

"Can I give you a word of advice?" Megan asked.

"I'm always open to suggestions."

"Hold on tight to him because if there's one thing I regret, it's letting go of him."

CHAPTER 10

Will stood on his tiptoes, trying to see if he could catch a glimpse of Katie among the throng of people who had gathered at Holly Wreath's town square to watch the Christmas tree lighting. There were so many faces that they all blurred together because none of them were Katie.

He wanted to swear but bit his tongue. He should have asked Katie to wait for him so they could go together. It'd been a while since he'd been to the tree lighting and, in his absence, it had grown exponentially. If he would have picked her up at her house, even if he was running late, the worst that would have happened would be that they missed watching the tree light up. Sure, it was a holiday tradition and was a sight to behold, but he would have been just as content curling up on the couch with her. It certainly would have made giving her a kiss or two a lot easier without people around.

He really should have asked her to go with him.

Kissing aside, he needed to unload about Megan. Her confession at the restaurant had left him unsettled in a way he couldn't shake. He'd had plenty of women longing for him even though he didn't reciprocate, but coming from Megan, the girl he once thought his whole world revolved around...it threw him off his game. Worse than Megan's confession was the fact that he felt like he hadn't been upfront about their lunch together. It didn't come up in conversation with Katie, and he'd purposefully kept himself from mentioning it. He didn't want her to worry that him eating with Megan meant anything. He'd needed to have that closure with Megan, and right when he thought he was going to get it, Megan threw the door wide open again.

Squeezing through a group of teenagers that were huddled together for warmth, he headed for the front of the crowd, toward the stage where a microphone and choir risers had been set up. If he had to guess where Katie would choose a spot, she'd want to get the full experience, front and center.

When he got there, Will turned to face the crowd, jumping a couple of times to see if he could spot her. Will knew he probably looked like an idiot, but that was irrelevant.

"Will!" He could hear Charlotte shouting his name. "Will!"

Looking to the right, he saw his sister and Harvey waving their arms to catch his attention. He excused himself as he wove through people, eventually crowding into a small space with them. Shaking Harvey's hand, Will gave him a quick evaluation. As much as he knew Charlotte was a grown woman and could handle herself, he was still her older brother and felt a certain amount of protectiveness for her. As far as he could tell, Harvey was a decent guy who wanted nothing more than to make Charlotte happy. If he ever heard any different, Will would have no problem showing him just what an older brother would do to a guy who'd hurt his sister.

"Are you looking for Katie?" Charlotte danced from one foot to the other, and held a gloved hand over her nose.

"I certainly wasn't looking for you," Will taunted.

Charlotte shoved him hard enough he had to apologize to the couple standing behind him for running into them. Making a face at his sister, she responded by sticking out her tongue.

"So have you seen her?" Will asked. "The tree lighting ceremony is going to start soon and I don't want to miss watching it with her."

Charlotte shook her head and snuggled up close to Harvey for extra warmth. "Have you tried calling her?"

"Only about five hundred times. Her phone is either on silent, or she can't hear it over the noise of the crowd."

"I sent her a text an hour before we got here, but she said she was going to hang back and wait for you. I can only imagine why." Charlotte made kissy noises at Will and he just rolled his eyes, but didn't deny a warm winter kiss with Katie to ward off the cold sounded like a great way to spend the evening.

"I'm going to keep looking then."

"My bet's on you not finding her. It's a literal needle in a haystack situation."

"If I have to borrow a megaphone and climb to the top of the Christmas tree to get her attention, I will."

"Aww, isn't that sweet?" Charlotte looked up to Harvey, who smiled and nodded. Did that man ever say a word?

"See you tomorrow at the parade, then," Will said, taking a step away.

Charlotte grabbed at his coat and tugged him back. "Hang on. There's something you need to know before you go."

Annoyed, Will sighed. "What is it?"

"If you break Katie's heart, even unintentionally, I will disown you. I swear, I'll choose her over you any day."

Will held up his hand to stop her. "Don't worry. Dad already gave me that lecture and I'm sure Mom will find time to give me one, too. I'm well-aware Katie is everyone's favorite by a longshot, and I wholeheartedly agree. If I screw things up, it's entirely on me."

"So there's nothing going on with Megan?"

Charlotte's question took Will aback. He hadn't expected her to be suspicious of him and Megan, though it made sense. He'd never left any question when they were dating that he was at Megan's beck and call, and when they broke up, he did nothing to hide his bitterness toward her.

He took a breath to slow his racing heart and stuck his hands in his pockets to hide that they were quivering. "What do you mean?"

"Last night, when I was giving Katie a makeover, Megan happened to come in."

"Katie let you give her a makeover? Please tell me you didn't do anything too drastic to my girlfriend."

Girlfriend. He hadn't called her that before, yet it felt so right.

Charlotte smirked at his choice of words, too. "You haven't seen her yet?"

"Nope. She had to work all day today, and I was working late into the night last night, so this tree lighting is the first chance we'll get to see each other."

"Try not to drool too much when you see her."

"I can't guarantee anything, but I'll try."

"Good. So, anyway. Megan." Charlotte pursed her lips. "I got the impression while I was trimming her hair that she still has a thing for you."

Will wanted to bury his face in his hands. Last year, if he and Megan had crossed paths and she'd confessed to him the way she had at lunch, he might have given her another shot, but after being with Katie, however brief, he'd been converted. Katie had shown him the light and he was fully committed to seeing where their relationship would go. Even the thought of going back to Austin made him squirm. He wasn't sure he could stand the distance so far away from her.

"Megan…she's complex. I'm not sure what she wants," Will said.

"The entire time she was in my chair, all we talked about was you."

Will let his shoulders rise and fall. "I'm sure it was because I'm the person you have in common. What else would you talk about?"

Charlotte shook her head and waved a pointer finger in front of his face. "Nope, that's not how it works. Women who come into the salon don't only talk to me about the people we both know. They talk about their exercise classes, what favorite book they've just finished, town gossip, the weather. All sorts of things. What tipped me off though is that Megan talked all about you. Not you and Katie."

"I see." Will grunted. "I didn't think she'd go telling everyone else that she still had a thing for me. She already told me."

Charlotte looked like she was going to choke on her own tongue. "She *told* you? When?"

"*Shh!*" Will hushed his sister. "I don't exactly want everyone in Holly Wreath knowing my business. I've enjoyed having a certain measure of anonymity here. I like not being in the tabloids."

"There aren't any tabloids in Holly Wreath. Or paparazzi for that matter."

"Tabloids, no, but there are plenty of gossips who do just as much damage."

Charlotte folded her arms. "When did Megan tell you this? Surely she didn't do it in front of Katie when she found you at church."

"No, she had some decency to do it in private." Will noticed the town mayor was talking with one of the tech crew, getting ready to get on stage to start the event. "We went to lunch on Wednesday to hash things out."

Charlotte's shock showed. "You did what?"

Her reaction made heat prickle at the back of Will's neck. "We had lunch. It was totally innocent."

"Did you tell Katie?"

Will couldn't find his voice. It was dawning on him with renewed urgency that he'd screwed up big time. "Not yet. I was planning on it, when everything was all settled with Megan. I don't want Katie worrying about anything."

"You dummy!" Charlotte slugged his shoulder. "Katie isn't an idiot. Part of why she came in on Thursday was because she was worried something was up with you. Guess what, genius? She figured it out. You were acting strange when you saw her Wednesday because you'd just gone to lunch with Megan right before you delivered the flowers."

"I'm not two-timing anyone, if that's what you're implying. Two people can have a conversation over a meal without it being romantic."

"Then why haven't you said anything to Katie about it?"

Charlotte was right. Will knew he'd painted himself into a corner and he was going to have a hard time getting himself out if he didn't fess up and come clean before he really made a mess of things.

"Okay, look. You're right that I probably shouldn't have kept Katie in the dark about it, but, honestly, I did it with the best of intentions. Megan means nothing to me anymore, but I needed closure. I'm totally and singularly committed to Katie. No one else even comes close. I'll tell her about my lunch with Megan as soon as I get the chance."

Charlotte pointed a finger at Will and poked him in the shoulder. "You'd better or you best believe I'll tell her. You're not going to start building your relationship on deception. That's a recipe for disaster."

"She's got a point," Harvey interjected.

He could speak.

"Alright. Do me a favor though and don't freak her out by blabbing to her before I have a chance to explain, okay?"

Charlotte sniffed. "Fine. But if I find out, so help me—"

"You don't have to worry about the 'what if' scenarios. I'll figure out a way to tell her without any of your help." Will hitched his thumb over his shoulder. "I'm going to go now. If I never find her, your fears are never going to be put to rest, are they?"

"Go." Charlotte shooed him away. "She's probably waiting for you with bated breath to come sweep her off her feet, though I'll never understand why."

"You of all people should know she has good taste."

Will grinned at his sister as he turned to hurry away as fast as he could through the swarm of people. He pulled his phone out of his pocket, trying Katie's number one more time, but with no luck. Picking up a jog, he skirted around the edge of the town square, his eyes darting back and forth.

And then he saw her.

He wasn't into sappy, romance movies where a man and woman were drawn together by an unseen magnetism, but finding Katie was the closest he'd ever felt to experiencing it. She was standing on the railing of the gazebo, scanning the crowd for him. Charlotte was right—the makeover she'd given her had only accentuated the best parts of her.

When Katie spotted Will, her entire face lit up with the kind of smile she seemed to save only for him. She waved him over and he jogged to the gazebo, offering to help her down. Reaching for him, he caught her by the waist and she wrapped her arms around him. He held her there, burying his face in her hair, savoring everything about being so close to her.

She kissed his cheek and murmured, "It feels like I haven't seen you in days."

"That's entirely too long, isn't it?" Will set her down on her feet and took her hand.

She guided them up to the gazebo, where she'd set her purse to save her spot. It was a little tight, but he didn't mind being pressed up against Katie as she held onto the railing, facing the tree.

"Sorry it took me so long to find you." Katie leaned back against him and he wrapped his arms around her, pulling her in closer. "I tried calling."

Katie looked up at him and cringed. "I forgot my phone at home, but didn't want to go back and get it since parking is almost impossible."

"That's alright. I found you now."

Katie turned around and buried her face in his chest, holding him tight around his waist. He rested his chin on top of her head and breathed deeply, relishing the soap and shampoo and a touch of perfume that lingered on her skin.

"You look amazing," Will murmured in her hair, "though I hope you didn't go changing yourself on my account. You looked gorgeous before Charlotte got her hands on you, too."

Katie tipped her head back. "You like it?"

"I do."

"Me, too. And for the record, I didn't change my look for you, but it may have been because of you. I think you've been a sort of catalyst to getting me out of my comfort zone, so I can try new things. I don't think that's bad."

"I know exactly how you feel."

Katie pressed her cheek against his chest again and sighed, her body relaxing against his. What Charlotte had admonished him to do ran on loop through his thoughts, affecting the speed of his heart.

Katie heard because she tipped her head back and smirked. "Your heart sounds like a jackhammer. Have something you want to get off your chest before your ribs crack from all the abuse?"

Will laughed at her observation. She never failed to surprise him with the way she could say what was on her mind without being offensive or pushy. Charlotte's stern voice sounded in his head once again, but he elbowed it to the background. He didn't want to ruin a perfectly good moment talking about Megan. There would be another time to come clean, when he could tell her without a horde of people with eavesdropping ears nearby.

He thought of what else could explain his racing pulse, and when he did, his heart went into double-time. He wanted to tell her something else that had been on his mind.

"Katie?"

She tilted her chin up to him, and she nibbled her lower lip, making her look all the more kissable. He indulged in a kiss that was deep and expressive, but always seemed too short.

"Katie, I don't want to scare you off, but there is something I've been meaning to tell you."

"There's not much you could do that would make me run. I'm not a skittish kind of girl."

Will brushed her hair off her brow and tucked it behind her ear. "I wanted to tell you that I think you're incredible, smart, and the most beautiful woman I've ever had the pleasure of knowing. I love you, Katie."

A fledgling smile tugged at Katie's lips until it entirely took over. "I've never understood why anyone would be scared away at another person's profession of love. What more is there to this mortal experience than to love and be loved? As for me, I've waited years to hear you say that to me."

Will tipped his forehead down to hers. "I hope your patience has been rewarded."

She kissed him again with her whole soul. It was enough to take away his breath and make him feel like he was totally powerless against her charms. "I've been meaning to tell you something as well."

"Oh, yeah?" Will furrowed his brow. "What's that?"

"I love you, too."

CHAPTER 11

Katie adjusted her legs, trying to get comfortable. The concrete curb under her rear end was unforgiving and she pulled her coat up to cover her nose to try to keep it from freezing. The relatively tepid weather they'd been having had gone straight to winter the day before, meaning the annual Saturday Christmas parade in Holly Wreath was going to be downright frigid. That didn't stop people from gathering to watch, though. Everyone brought enough blankets and knit hats and did their best to sit in the sun to catch some of its warmth. Already, Katie could hear from the downtown parking lot where the parade participants were gathering, that on the main strip, a crowd was already packing in, practically erupting with excitement. It made huddling in the cold worth it.

"Cold?" Will asked as he returned with a pair of hot apple ciders steaming in a drink carrier, and two flaky pastries wrapped in a bag.

Katie wrinkled her nose and stared at the cup of cider, conflicted about what to do.

"Is something the matter?" Will asked.

"You're super sweet offering breakfast…"

"But?"

"I don't really like hot cider. And by really, I mean it's gross."

Will blinked at her confession and retracted his hand. Chuckling, he awkwardly set down the drinks and brushed off his hands like he'd been holding a clod of manure instead of food. "Well, I learned something new today."

"I like it cold but something about it being heated up…" Katie shivered under her coat as a nip of air snuck down her neck. "You know what? I'm going to give it a try. Maybe I've grown out of my aversion and, if nothing else, it'll warm me up. This breakfast just might save me. Thanks for bringing it."

Will handed her one and held up his cup. "Cheers. And next time, I'll stick to hot chocolate."

She gave him a quick peck on the cheek. "I do appreciate it. I wasn't expecting anything more than a kiss from you this morning as you sent me off on the parade."

"That I can deliver." He pulled her close with one arm and kissed her straight on the mouth, eliciting a few catcalls from the high school kids a couple spots in front of them in the parade lineup.

Katie pretended like she didn't care, but turned away, flustered that anyone had been watching. "I just wish it was even five degrees warmer. The weatherman promised a cold morning but I mean, come on. We're not in the arctic."

Will drew her close again in a side hug, vigorously running his hand up and down her arm. "It probably doesn't help that we're in the shadow of the buildings back here. Once the parade starts and you get some direct rays, it won't be so bad."

She set her drink down on the wagon where she'd be

riding with the rest of the dental office staff. "I'm sure you're right." Katie checked the time on her phone and took a bite of her pastry. "Only about half an hour before it begins. I can make it."

A nearby group of 4-H kids had begun unloading their haltered alpacas, dressing them in funny outfits. A pair of them were Santa and Mrs. Claus, and judging by the enormous pointy ears and hats, the rest were supposed to be their Christmas elves. None of the animals seemed particularly impressed with their costumes, but they were still cooperative. Ahead of them was the Holly Wreath High School marching band, all blowing through their instruments to try and keep them warm and in tune, and the Shriners in their tiny cars were already entertaining everyone as they zipped around an open space. Katie had already walked the lineup, stopping to talk to several of her friends she'd recognized. Holly Wreath's Christmas parade might be modest compared to other bigger city's shows, but the enthusiasm by the participants and crowd was equally infectious.

Taking a sip of steaming hot cider, Will looked around the parking area. "Want to go stand over by those bushes? The sun's already hitting them."

"Sure. Between that and this apple cider, I might be able to stave off hypothermia."

Katie grabbed her breakfast and led the way to the shaggy yew bushes where the golden sunlight had already reached. The second she stepped into the sunshine, she closed her eyes and relished the warmth, but mid-stride, she knew something was wrong. Her foot slipped out from under her and she could feel herself losing her balance in a way she knew she wasn't going to be able to recover from.

Her apple cider flew out of her hand and a scream ripped out of her throat. Before she hit the ground with a hard thump, Will's strong arms caught her and took the brunt of the momentum, cushioning her from the unforgiving cobblestone.

In an instant, Katie rolled off of him and was on her knees with her hands on his cheeks. "Will? Are you alright?"

His eyes fluttered open and he sat up gingerly, brushing his hands down his face and coat. He was soaked with her cider. "If you didn't want to drink the apple cider I brought, you could have said no thanks and left it at that."

Any heat that was in Katie's face drained and she hid her embarrassment behind her hands. Peeking between her fingers, she apologized. "I'm so sorry. I should have had a tighter grip on my drink and watched where I was going. I walked right onto that patch of ice and now you're soaked."

Will chuckled and kissed her cheek, then ran his hand down her jawline. She leaned into his touch and tried to keep the tears from falling. "Hey. I'll live. I was a wrestler in high school, remember? We learned how to fall the right way so we didn't get hurt."

"I didn't break your tailbone?"

"Not even a scratch. Just a little wet." He winked at Katie and stood up, grabbing her by the elbows and putting her on her feet. "There. No worse for..."

Will's eyes widened and a silly grin wobbled on his lips.

"What is it?" Katie asked. "Oh, my goodness. You did get hurt, didn't you? I can drive you to the nearest urgent care and—"

Will held up his hand. "I almost wish a medical emergency was the problem but, unfortunately, it's a much more delicate matter. You don't happen to have a sewing kit on you by chance, do you? Or a bunch of safety pins?"

"No. Sorry. Why—?"

"My heroic act cost me my pants. It seems I've split them all the way down my backside."

Katie sputtered and tried to restrain a laugh but it was

useless. Will held both hands on his backside, grinning at how Katie had doubled over, clutching her sides as she tried to stop herself.

"I'm so sorry. This morning is a total disaster. Why don't you sit down and I'll go find a store for some replacement pants?"

"No, it's alright. You're the one in the parade and I'd hate for you to miss it. I'll just run around the corner. Surely there's one of the boutiques on main street that's got something I can use. I'll be back in a couple minutes."

Katie watched him go, pinching her lips together as long as she could until laughter overtook her again. Will had always been so cool and collected, and while he definitely handled the mortifying situation better than she would have, it was hilarious to watch him jogging into the crowd with both hands clutching his rear end.

Sitting down on the curb by the bushes, Katie finished her pastry and made sure to toss her trash in a nearby garbage can. With fifteen minutes still to go until the parade even started, she tightened her hood around her, bowed her head, and curled up as tight as she could.

"Ho, ho, ho!"

Snapping her head up, she squinted against the rising sun to see Will dressed in a red velvet Santa suit. She would have laughed if she wasn't so caught off guard by his choice of outfit.

"Where did you find a Santa suit?" she asked, unable to keep her mouth from hanging open.

"I tried a couple of the clothing stores on main street, but everything is closed until after the parade. There was one toy store open and I convinced the owner to sell me the suit off his mannequin. I figured it was better than walking around with my boxers exposed."

A snorting laugh came out of Katie. "You are nothing if not resourceful."

"Oh, it gets better." Will held up a large plastic sack. "I got the matching Mrs. Claus suit."

Katie played innocent. "For who?"

"For you, my dear."

Katie wrapped her coat tighter around herself. "It's cute that you're dressed up as Santa, but don't you think for a second I'm going to sacrifice my coat so I can squeeze into an itty bitty Mrs. Claus outfit."

Will pulled out the dress. The red velvet was lined with fluffy white at the sleeves, and a white half-apron with lace along the edges was sewn around the waist. "No need to ditch your coat. Their Mrs. Claus was rather plump, so it should fit right over the top of your coat. Bonus extra layer."

Katie eyed Will as a smile crept across her lips. "How'd I get so lucky?"

"I wouldn't particularly call you lucky this morning, what with the ice and all."

"No, I mean with you. Most guys would have rather worn ripped jeans than be silly and put on a Santa outfit. I take it as a very good sign that you don't take yourself too seriously."

Katie slid the dress over her head and adjusted it until everything was straightened out and comfortable. Will ran the zipper up her back for her and she held up her hands for his approval.

Will set Mrs. Claus' wig and hat on Katie's head. "Life's too short not to have fun, don't you think? But I consider myself the lucky one to have landed you. Do you know how many women there are out there that would be too self-conscious or would be proverbial sticks in the mud rather than dress up like a plump Mrs. Claus?" Katie shook her head. "A lot. Yet I managed to find one who somehow pulls it off and still looks beautiful."

A shrill whistle rang in the air, signaling the start of the parade. Taking Will's hand, they strolled back to the dental clinic's tractor and wagon. They were still halfway back in the lineup and it would be a while before they would be moving.

"How's Charlotte been treating you now that she knows we're dating?" Katie asked, looking up into Will's face. "She says she's happy for me, but I want to know if she's secretly upset about it and doesn't want me to know."

She'd never get tired of gazing at him. His charisma and charm were only enhanced by the fact he was so handsome, with a chiseled jawline and strong nose—even if most of his face was covered by a white, curly beard. And his eyes—they seemed to glow golden as they caught the sunlight.

"Why would she be upset that you're seeing me?" Will wrapped a reassuring arm around her shoulder.

"I dunno. If I was in the same situation, I might've thought it was weird to have my brother and best friend dating. I mean, what if it didn't work out? That'd be a hard position to be in. Charlotte would always be caught in the middle."

"We have already thoroughly established that everyone in my family loves you more than me. Heck, the whole town does."

"I don't know about that. Megan sure thinks highly of you."

The second Katie blurted Megan's name, she wanted to take it back. Will hadn't given Katie any reason to doubt and she didn't need to let any lingering insecurities drive a wedge between her and Will. She'd seen enough couple's relationships ruined by jealousy and false accusations to know it was a dangerous path to entertain.

Will kissed her temple. "Don't worry about Megan. She's always going to be a part of my past, but I'm choosing you for my future. As for Charlotte, I'm pretty sure she's already collecting wedding magazines."

"For her or me?"

"Probably both. How would you feel about a double wedding with Charlotte and Harvey?"

Katie knew he was joking, but a flutter tickled her stomach. She could almost imagine what it would be like to walk down the aisle to a waiting William Ryan. If she wanted big and splashy or quiet and cozy, she knew he would give it to her.

Yes, she'd had more than one immature daydream growing up about marrying Will. She was getting ahead of herself by a longshot, but she liked imagining it all the same.

"I have a feeling Charlotte would want her own special day. I could do back to back though," Katie said with a smirk.

"I'm sure she'll insist on any firstborn child being named after her, too. You know, for benevolently encouraging our relationship rather than putting a stop to it."

"Middle name. Maybe." Will chuckled and Katie wanted to, but there was a tiny problem to her fantasy. "If only you lived here instead of Austin."

Will stopped Katie and pulled her around to face him. "I know that's sort of a stumbling block to our relationship, but I think there's more going for us than you recognize."

"Is that so?"

"Yeah, I do. For example, there's technology. It's not like moving across the plains as a pioneer, knowing you're never going to see that person again."

"Sure, but it's a little difficult to kiss over the phone, don't you think?"

That earned Katie another chortle. "True, but there are

also other luxuries I've become accustomed to thanks to my financial standing."

"You're planning on using your business jet to fly back and forth?"

"That's definitely one of the benefits of owning a jet, yes. Plus, I could always send it to pick you up and you could join me in Austin or wherever I have to go for an event. You're going to be my plus-one from now on, aren't you?"

Katie looked at him through downturned lashes. "I would like to do some traveling. I haven't gotten to see as much of the world as I'd like."

"I think what's really going to keep us afloat is passion."

Katie dropped her head, her laugh tinged with cynicism. "You and passion. It takes more than that to keep a relationship alive, you know."

"Sure," Will agreed with a shrug, "but passion is the heartbeat of a couple. Sometimes it races, sometimes it's slow and steady, but once it stops, they might as well dig a grave."

"Okay, that's pretty profound."

"Make sure you tell Charlotte that. She's positive I'm a mindless oaf."

"Isn't that what all sisters are supposed to think of their brothers? I wouldn't know as an only child."

At the wagon she was supposed to be riding, Katie stopped short. She didn't want to end her time with Will, even if it was only temporarily. Yes, he'd made sure in no uncertain terms that he wanted to see her as much as possible when he went back to Austin, but it wouldn't be the same. There wouldn't be any impromptu lunches, no bumping into each other when they were in town, no surprise flowers hand delivered by him. She sighed heavily, but hid it by faking a yawn.

"You're not getting tired already, are you?" Will asked, poking her in the ribs.

She swatted his hand away. "Careful. I happen to have it on good authority that you're extremely ticklish and I will not hesitate to use that knowledge against you."

He held up his hands as a show of submission. "Alright, alright. Point taken."

"As for tired, maybe a little. I was up pretty early to get everything set up for the parade. I had to run to the office to get the stuff we're tossing for the parade."

"Candy?"

"No." Katie shook her head. "Toothbrushes. Everyone else will already be tossing candy."

Will rolled his eyes and chuckled, holding his belly like he was the real Kris Kringle. "I should have guessed."

"They make excellent business cards for when all the little kids come in with cavities."

"Well, lame parade gift aside, you'd better make sure you get a good nap before the social tonight."

Katie playfully tugged on his beard. "And why's that?"

"Because I'm not taking you home until they kick us out the door."

"Are you big into dancing? Because other than dinner, I think that's all there is."

Will took Katie in his arms and spun her around, dancing a few steps around the parking lot with her. "I'll have you know I took ballroom dancing lessons with another girl I dated. It was more fun than I thought it would be and it turns out that I've got decent rhythm."

"Then I accept your invitation to dance until we can't stand on our feet any longer. Though if you must know, I went shopping with Charlotte yesterday after work and she insisted I wear high heels. It's not often that I wear them, so there's no guarantee I won't totally biff it."

"I think I've already proven I'm good at catching you and

if I'm not slipping on ice too, I bet I can even make you look good while you're falling."

"Katie? Is that you?" Dr. Hamilton, Katie's boss and owner of the dental clinic, squinted at her from the wagon bed. She nodded. "Where'd you get the outfit from?"

Pointing to Will, she said, "Last minute outfit change thanks to my..."

"Boyfriend, sir." Will held out his hand and introduced himself. "Will Ryan."

"Ah, yes. Carol and Roger's boy. They said you were back in town. Hope you're enjoying your time with Katie."

Will winked inconspicuously at Katie. "I definitely am, sir."

"Well, good. Enjoy being young while you can, but for now, it's time to get this show on the road." Dr. Hamilton put up the hood of his costume—a red toothbrush with bristles sprouting around his head.

Katie and Will exchanged a look, keeping their sniggering hidden behind pinched lips.

Helping Katie up to the wagon, Dr. Hamilton motioned for Will to join them. "Can't very well have Mrs. Claus without Santa, can we? Have you got the time, Will?"

"For Katie? Always."

Will climbed up onto the wagon and he took his place next to Katie as the big red tractor pulling them belched out a ball of black smoke and roared to life. Wrapping his arm low on her waist, he drew Katie next to him. Even under the thick suit, she could feel his steady breathing, and his after-shave was just as scrumptiously tempting as always. Despite her best efforts, she was still chilled to the bone and tired from the early morning, but she couldn't think of a time when she was happier. Life was definitely looking up.

"Can you do me a favor?" Will murmured into her ear for only her to hear.

She could hardly breathe out the word. "Anything."

"I keep falling for you, over and over, every time we're together. Promise you'll catch me, too?"

Placing a gentle kiss on his lips, she held his face in her hands. "Always."

CHAPTER 12

W ill had been to enough swanky parties in his life that he knew what to expect at Holly Wreath's Christmas Social. He'd had his personal assistant back in Austin ship his tux out the morning after he'd convinced Katie to go with him, and even if it was overkill, he wanted the evening to be special for her. He knew he looked good in his custom made, jet black tuxedo, and he was going to make sure she was the envy of every woman there.

As confident as he felt, he had about melted when he'd gone to Katie's door to pick her up. She answered and it took him a moment to soak her all in. She wore her hair in a simple bun low on the nape of her neck with a few strands loose by her ears, and a pale pink dress that fit her figure like a glove. She'd even put on the dreaded heels Charlotte had helped her pick out. It didn't escape his notice that they made her legs look amazing. She was ravishing and angelic, all in one.

"Do you want to find our seats first, or should we work up an appetite on the dance floor?" he asked her as they handed over their winter things at the coat check. "I'm perfectly happy doing whatever you want."

"How about a dance or two? I'm curious if you really can live up to your reputation for dancing or if you're all talk."

Will grinned wickedly and led her to the dance floor, where he spun her like he had in her Mrs. Claus outfit, but, without the extra bulk, he was able to press her close to him. Dipping her back, he enjoyed the elation on her face.

He whispered into her ear, "I guarantee I'm as good as I say I am."

She was breathless and pink in the cheeks as he lifted her back to her feet. The small diamond pendant she wore sparkled near her collarbone and her matching earrings caught the light. He was struck all over again at how attractive she was. It was amazing how quickly they'd gotten into a rhythm with each other. She was comfortable, but not boring, and she had a way of setting all his fantasies in motion. Before he'd come back to Holly Wreath, he'd been so caught up in living in the moment that he rarely gave thought to the future. With Katie, time seemed to stretch out before him in the best of ways.

Whisking her around the dance floor, he stopped short of a table off to the left. Megan was sitting alone, her pointer finger tangled in her hair as she stared at him. A sad smile appeared and she held up her hand and twiddled her fingers. Will nodded in acknowledgement but before Katie noticed his attention had been temporarily distracted by his ex, he swept her back to the other end of the dance floor.

When the song ended and an upbeat version of *Jingle Bell Rock* began playing, Will moved Katie off to the side to give other couples more space.

Pressing her hand to her chest, she panted slightly. "Okay, you have me totally convinced. You are an amazing dancer. I bet you're going to end up on one of those televised dancing competitions."

"Oh, no I won't. I don't mind if you know that I can dance, but I have several friends who would laugh me to scorn if they knew I could waltz. I'd never hear the end of it."

"I'm kind of shocked that a guy like you cares what other people think of him."

Will tugged at the lapels of his tux jacket to adjust it. "It might surprise you to know that I don't have as thick of skin as it sometimes may seem."

"That's probably a good thing. I don't think it's healthy for anyone not to care, as long as they aren't paralyzed by any resulting fear."

Will clasped her wrist and kissed her hand. "Can I say how much I love the way you think?"

"You'd get no complaints from me. Compliment away."

Will beamed at her. With her by his side, he felt like the luckiest man on the planet. Glancing across the town hall, he caught another glimpse of Megan. He knew he needed to come clean with Katie about their lunch, not because he thought he'd done anything wrong in meeting with her, other than keeping it a secret. It should have been a point of conversation between Katie and him before he'd gone. Will was sure he'd feel the same way if Katie had gone out with Rex. Not that it was even a remote possibility since Rex had already proven himself a loser.

"Oh, no," Katie muttered under her breath. Holding her hand up over her face, she was clearly trying to hide herself.

"What?"

"Rex at two o'clock."

Will straightened himself and looked over Katie's head. Sure enough, Rex was trying to impress a bunch of people at a table as he leaned over, his arms across the back of two women's chairs who looked utterly annoyed, telling a story that only he seemed to be interested in hearing.

"Don't let him see you!" she hissed. "What is it with you and looking when you should be ducking your head?"

"I'm not intimidated by him."

"I'm not either, but if he sees you, he'll know I'm the one standing next to you."

"He wouldn't try anything while he knows we're together." Will took her hand in his to make a point.

"You remember how he behaved when we were getting tacos? Yes, he very much would try to swoop in. As earnestly as I put my trust in you, I wouldn't put it past Rex to be unable to get it through his thick head that I genuinely, truly am not going to go back to him." Katie peeked out from behind her hand, immediately jerking it back in place. "Crud. He's walking this way. I think he saw me."

Will glanced over again, a look of determination on his face. "I'll tell him to go away in a way that Rex won't misunderstand."

A nervous giggle bubbled out of her. "As much as I appreciate the gesture, I'd rather you not. I remember how you chased down one of Charlotte's boyfriends in the school parking lot, threatening to pummel him when you caught them making out. I was sure you were going to get arrested."

Will smirked. "You remember that?"

"It was like watching a high school soap opera unfold right in front of me. Very dramatic."

"That was a long time ago when hormones made a person unpredictable at best. I'll have you know I have a clean criminal record. Not even a parking ticket."

Katie moved to the other side of Will and he did his best to conceal her by turning his back to Rex to block his view. If they were lucky, Rex wouldn't notice she was there and would move past.

"Good for you," Katie pat Will on the chest. "I think it would be a good idea not to start tonight because if you punched him in the face, as flattering as that might be, I don't want you to end up in jail. I guarantee Rex's pride would be hurt more than anything and he'd press charges."

"Don't worry. I have an entire team of good lawyers."

"It's not that."

"What is it then?"

"I'd have to find myself a ride home."

Chuckling, Will guided Katie by her elbow to a darker corner, blocked by a pillar twinkling with strands of white lights intertwined with garland. "So glad to know you'd be concerned about me."

"Let's just not deck anyone tonight, either of us. I don't want you to go to jail and I don't want to have to find a ride home."

"Deal."

Leaning out from behind the pillar, Will spied Rex. He'd zeroed in on them and a sly smile fixed on his face.

"Maybe you should go powder your nose," Will said softly. The revulsion in Katie's face was almost laughable, but Will knew it wasn't the time to tease. "I don't mean I think you need it, but maybe it'll give you a chance to escape Rex and he'll move on past. If he won't take no for an answer, maybe we can elude him."

"Alright," Katie agreed. "Don't have too much fun without me."

"Never."

Pressing an earnest kiss to Will's mouth, Katie was the first to back away. Her fingers slipped out of his hand, and immediately, the cogs in his mind started turning. Running from Rex wasn't the way he wanted to spend his special evening with Katie, but Will wasn't sure how to get rid of her ex that wouldn't draw attention, not that he would mind putting his fist to Rex's face to get his point across. Katie was right though. It would be bad PR for his company and it probably wouldn't deter Rex as effectively as he'd like.

Will watched Katie skirt the edge of the room to the restrooms, keeping a careful watch for Rex, and disappear inside. She was safe, at least momentarily, from Rex's advances, but without her, Will felt a little lost himself.

"Hey."

Will looked over his shoulder to where Megan was approaching. She must have seen Katie leave and decided to make her move. The thought made Will tense and his blood pressure skyrocket. She might have been infinitely more amazing than Rex, but she had the same problem as him—she couldn't seem to take no for an answer.

"Hi," Will said, slipping his hands into his trouser pockets. If it kept Megan from casually brushing her skin against his, it was worth the protection of appearing standoffish. "Enjoying yourself tonight?"

"Yeah. I mean, it's a lot more fun than I remember it being. Probably because I'm more grown up now. Maybe that means I'm becoming a bore."

Laughing softly, Will shook his head. "You're not boring."

"You know what would make this party even more fun?"

"A life-sized ice sculpture of Santa?"

A peal of laughter came from Megan and for the first time since they'd talked at the Italian restaurant, there wasn't a trace of grief in her eyes. "You always were such a joker. Can you imagine how tacky that would be? No, a dance partner would make this night a heck of a lot more enjoyable."

She held out her hand, but Will only stared at it like she was offering him a handshake with a rattlesnake. He looked back at the restroom, wondering how long Katie was going to hide out. Maybe he should go wait for her over there when she did emerge.

"Come on, Will," Megan coaxed. "For old time's sake."

Will resisted, though he didn't want to be cruel. He'd moved on a long time ago and didn't harbor any resentment toward her either, even if she had residual doubts about missing him. He could let her down gently, but maintain that he was no longer interested. It would be a kindness not to leave her with even a glimmer of hope.

"One dance," he said firmly.

Megan schooled her smile and accepted his conditions. They found their way to the center of the dance floor, rocking back and forth to the slow, soulful jazz song that was playing. He spotted his parents dancing near Charlotte and Harvey, talking while they swayed. He moved Megan away from them, feeling trapped by the situation he'd found himself in. He was walking on eggshells and he didn't like it one bit.

Will couldn't think of a single thing to say that wouldn't end up navigating the conversation right back to where he didn't want it to go. As far as Will was concerned, anything Megan might want to say to convince him to change his mind was irrelevant. He looked forward to when she'd leave Holly Wreath and go back to California where the chances of them ever crossing paths again were very slim.

"Will, we need to talk."

So much for ignoring the elephant in the room. "I'm not sure there's anything that needs to be said."

Megan stopped swaying. "Yes, it does."

"You were pretty clear about it over lunch, and so was I."

"There's more I need to add."

"Fine." Will shoved a hand through his hair. "Do you want to go sit at your table?"

"And let my mom listen in on our conversation? Hard pass."

"Fair enough," Will said. "Go ahead, then. You might as

well say what's on your mind before I need to get back to my date."

Megan winced. The words were cutting, but he'd meant them to be. He was with Katie now. Though Megan had hurt him, she took his hand again and rested her other on his shoulder. He did the same and they started rocking back and forth again.

"I just…wanted to apologize to you. For Wednesday."

"Apology accepted."

Megan pounded a fist on his chest in frustration. "No. I don't want a flippant, indifferent acceptance. I feel like I need to explain myself."

"Alright. I'm listening."

Megan's eyes flitted around the room and she blinked back tears that she was determined to keep from falling. "What I said on Wednesday, I did mean it. I still think you're one of my greatest regrets, but what's done is done."

"I—"

"Wait. Don't interrupt or I won't be able to get through it without bawling."

Will nodded silently. He'd never seen her this torn up, and he wanted to give her the chance to unload. As a friend, he could do that for her.

"In California," Megan sniffled, "I'm actually seeing someone."

"Yeah? What's his name?"

"Sam. And he's a great guy. Loyal, dependable…you know the type. He is wonderful."

Will hesitated, shaking his head as he tried to make sense of her concern. "I'm sorry. I'm not understanding what you're worried about."

Megan laughed and tipped her head back as a single tear rolled down her cheek. "It doesn't make sense, does it? It's so stupid. When I say it out loud, I realize how dumb I'm being."

"Are you worried that you're not good enough for Sam?"

Pressing her pink lips together, Megan nodded. "I can't believe I turned down a marriage proposal from him because the thought of being a ball and chain to him scared me so much that I couldn't say yes."

"Hey," Will said. "Hold on. Can I say something?"

"Go for it. Tell me how rotten I am."

"That's not at all what I was thinking."

"Well, it couldn't have been very kind. I was so horrible to you and that's the last impression you had of me. Not exactly stellar."

"Yeah, things didn't work out for us. That's okay. We had some good times, but we were so young. It was a stepping stone for both of us that led to growth. We've both found wonderful people to be with. There's no shame in that."

"Katie is a sweetheart. She's so much better for you than I ever was."

"She is wonderful, but that's not the point I'm trying to make," Will said, running his hand down his cheeks as he tried to figure out how to word what he was thinking. "You're not Katie and I'm not trying to compare her to you. In your own right, you're an amazing woman. Smart and funny and so clever. Sam would be an idiot to pass you up. I don't even know Sam, but I guarantee that on every level, you'd be his equal."

Megan rested her head on Will's shoulder, wiping away another tear. "Thanks. I think I needed to hear that from an unbiased source. My dad's told me that a hundred times, but somehow, it didn't register. What dad doesn't think his daughter is infinitely better than any guy she might marry?"

"Then let me add my vote of confidence in your character to his opinion. Sam's a lucky guy."

Megan nodded, pressing her lips tightly to contain another sob. "I'm not sure what I'm going to do now that I've messed everything up. For the longest time, I was so confused. I was so madly in love with him, then he told me he wanted to marry me, and I freaked out and escaped to Holly Wreath, the tiniest town in Wyoming, where he'll never find me. Seeing you tangled all my already confusing emotions into even more of a mess, and then I had to really screw up by telling you I thought I still had feelings for you. Gosh, I am such a wreck."

"It's fine. Everything works out in the end."

"Does it?" Megan's tears stopped and she let out a shuddering sigh. "I feel like I keep getting outwitted by life because I don't know what to expect next."

"That's kind of the fun of life, isn't it? It's always throwing curveballs at us. Keeps everyone on their toes, I think."

"I didn't mess anything up between you and Katie, did I? That might be the thing that does me in if I find out that I ruined what you two have. I know you just started dating, but I can tell how infatuated you are with her. That's how I feel about Sam. Of course, when I'm not busy panicking."

"No. I haven't said anything to Katie." Will amended, "Yet."

"Good. Don't let go of that girl if you can. I've never seen you so happy, even when you're posing on the cover of magazines and trying to fake it for everyone. She adds a sparkle to your eye."

"Tell you what. I'll do my best to keep Katie happy, but you have to do the same for Sam. I don't know how things are going to work for the two of you, but if he's as great as you say he is, then give him the benefit of the doubt. Explain your concerns. If he loves you, he'll understand and can wait for you to be ready. If not, well, then at least you know before you've taken any big, committed steps."

Megan nodded, sighing against his shoulder. "I'm going to call him tonight."

"Good."

Will felt a weight lifted from him, knowing he'd helped Megan sort through the complexities of life and reassured that he wasn't breaking her heart by rejecting her. Returning to Holly Wreath had been therapeutic for him, too, and he was glad that he wasn't carrying around any more excess baggage that, for years, he'd attributed to Megan. It was freeing to forgive and move on.

The song drew to a close, and his thoughts turned back to Katie. Rex was nowhere to be seen, and if she was lucky, she'd be able to escape and come back to Will unnoticed. He was ready to have her in his arms for the rest of the evening.

The only problem was she was already standing at the edge of the dance floor. She'd spotted Will dancing with Megan, and from a distance, it must have looked all wrong. With a glare of contempt contorting her features, Will knew she was livid and she wasn't going to hold back.

CHAPTER 13

Counting to a hundred a couple of times, Katie figured it would be safe to leave the women's restroom. She checked her makeup, but it was still in place—they hadn't eaten anything and though her dance with Will was lively, she hadn't quite worked up a sweat and though their last kiss was passionate, she was impressed her lipstick was still where it was supposed to be. She made a mental note to buy more of it. If it didn't smudge after kissing Will like that, it had to be quality. Pushing open the bathroom door, she surveyed the room through the crack. Rex was nowhere to be seen.

She let go of a breath she'd been holding, relieved that Rex had moved on, and stepped back out into the party. As obnoxious as Rex could be, it was nice that he was predictable. He was easily distracted, which meant he wasn't one to linger. Katie was probably all but a fleeting thought.

"Katie!" Charlotte squealed as she floated over. She looked fantastic in a bold red dress that trailed behind her like a cloud. She took Katie's hands in hers and evaluated

Katie, dressed in the outfit she'd helped her choose from the boutique. "You're so beautiful."

"I was just thinking the same thing of you. I hope Harvey knows how blessed he is."

Searching around the room, Charlotte asked, "Where's Will?"

"I'm not sure. I had to maneuver into the women's restroom to avoid Rex."

Charlotte's eyes rolled back as she groaned. "Ugh. He's here?"

"How could he miss it? So many pretty ladies to hit on."

"Don't hesitate to tell me if he's bothering you. I have no reservations about slapping him."

Katie smothered her laugh with her hand so it wouldn't be too loud. "Don't worry. Your brother already offered to deck him if needed, so I think I'm covered."

"Good," Charlotte said with a curt nod. "I'm going to run to the little girl's room. Meet me back at our table?"

"Where are we?"

"Second row from the front, off to the left. I think my parents went to go sit down. They're supposed to be starting dinner in a couple of minutes and Mom forgot how much she hates wearing heels."

Katie and Charlotte parted and Katie strolled toward the dance floor, still unsure of where Will had disappeared to. There were plenty of people here that he'd know from childhood that he may have gone to chat with, but Katie had been hoping he'd be waiting for her.

"Well, hello there, pretty lady."

Revulsion seeped into Katie and the muscles at the base of her neck tightened. Rex had found her, despite her best efforts to avoid him. It was inevitable, anyway. She probably would have run into him one way or another during the social. Rolling her neck to relax, she put on a bright smile and spun around to face him. He took a step forward, she took three steps back.

"Hello, Rex." She glanced at the woman holding his hand. He was here with a date and still trying to schmooze other women? Rex officially bottomed out as her least favorite person. "Who is this with you tonight?"

"Amanda Jo," Rex said proudly, wrapping his arm tightly around her slender waist. She wore a purple dress that set off her orange spray tan, and her voluminous hair added at least three inches to her height.

"Pleasure to meet you, Amanda Jo." Shaking her hand, Katie wondered where on earth Rex had found someone to accompany him. "If you'll excuse me, I need to get back to my date."

"Will?" Rex's words sounded slurred as he spoke and the faint smell of alcohol wafted from him. She also didn't appreciate the way his eyes trickled down her body. He ran the back of his hand across the corner of his mouth. Was he drooling over her? "I didn't know he was your date."

Katie grit her teeth until her jaw hurt. "I told you he was at the Tex Mex Oasis, remember?"

"I know that's what you said. But if he's your date, why's he dancing with his ex?"

Katie blinked, shaking her head and wondering if she'd heard right. "Excuse me?"

"Last I saw, he was out on the dance floor with that buxom, blue-eyed beauty, Megan," Rex said, his murky eyes growing harder as he recognized the panic setting in Katie. He knew he'd hit a nerve.

"Rex!" Amanda Jo squealed. "You're going to get slapped on the mouth if you don't quit ogling other women."

Katie bit her tongue, stopping herself from telling Amanda Jo she was going to have to get in line.

"Sorry, babe." He kissed her cheek. "Don't forget, you're the most beautiful one here."

Katie had no idea if Rex was telling the truth—she wouldn't put it past him to spin tales to try and sew a seed of doubt in hopes she'd come running back to him—but she wanted to be back in the security of Will's arms. Rex officially had made her skin crawl.

"If you'll excuse me." Katie gave them a small smile as she left.

"If it doesn't work out with you and Will, give me a call!" Rex shouted.

Katie's cheeks burned and, though she tried to ignore him, people would know he'd been talking to her. There was absolutely no way she would ever willingly associate with Rex, but that didn't mean everyone else knew it.

She wove through the tables, barely hearing anything as the sound of blood rushing in her ears muffled everything outside her own head. Katie wasn't used to living in a place of doubt, but with her relationship with Will so new, and knowing he was a desirable bachelor, all topped off with feeling like she was in competition with a perfect, untouchable ex, panic gripped Katie with its icy, unyielding fingers.

A few people caught her to chat as she walked and she did her best to be engaging, but her efforts were paltry at best. Stopping at the edge of the parquet dance floor, Katie froze. Through the other couples bobbing around, obscuring her line of sight, she caught a very distinct view of Will. Megan's head was resting on his shoulder.

Any warm, fuzzy feelings she'd had when they'd arrived swiftly died, leaving her with an empty cavern in her chest. Her heart ached worse than if she'd been kicked by an angry mule. She was metaphorically down for the count. It hadn't even been five measly minutes that she'd been gone before Megan swooped in and made her move. Feeling her nails dig into the palms of her hands, she trembled with rage. The worst part of all of it was that Will was a willing participant in all of it. He was a two-timing sleaze, just like some of the media outlets painted him out to be and right in front of her; Katie had her very own proof.

Someone stood next to Katie and she glanced sideways at them. It was Piper, a woman she'd known her whole life and one of the town's favorite doctors. She was beaming next to Rudger, a quiet cowboy with eyes only for Piper. Katie had met Rudger when she was conversing with Piper at the parade, and it was clear there was something special between them.

The whole day had been fractured, and the parade—before she was so angry at Will she could barely see—felt like eons ago. She'd been glad to see Piper so content with Rudger, but now, it was a slap in the face. Why did Piper get to find her special someone while Katie was stuck watching her world crumble around her? Katie shook her head. She couldn't let her mind wander down that dark path. She'd learned while watching her mother slowly slip away from her as the cancer ravaged her body that Katie couldn't afford to think life was unfair. The experiences in it were bitter enough. She didn't need to make it worse by poisoning her mind with jealousy for the perfect lives other people appeared to have. She knew it was all an illusion and that everyone was struggling.

"If you'll excuse me, I need to speak with someone." Katie tried to smile at Olivia and Heather, but the effort was too much.

Katie watched Will and Megan for a moment, unsure of what to do. If she left without saying a word, it'd let Will off the hook. Katie wasn't one for confrontation, either. She liked being a peacemaker. What she didn't like was being walked all over and made a fool.

Before her mind had been made up, her feet started walking through the dancing couples, straight to Megan and Will. She had no idea what she was going to say, but Will was going to know that he'd just lost the best thing that had ever happened to him.

Megan was the first to notice her. She lifted her head off his shoulder and her eyes widened while Katie's narrowed into slits. Megan's reaction alerted Will and he dropped Megan like a hot potato.

"Katie," he said as he ran his hand through his hair. "Did you make it out of there without running into Rex?"

Katie's laugh was acrid. "Seriously? That's what you're going to lead with?"

Will shifted on his feet. "What are you talking about?"

"You abandoned me, leaving me to fend for myself—that's right. Rex was there waiting and I had the pleasure of deflecting his advances all by myself."

"Geez, I'm sorry, Katie. I thought he'd lost interest and moved on," Will said.

"He didn't. As uncomfortable as that all was, it was nothing compared to seeing you slow dance with your ex."

"This isn't what it looks like." Megan tried to help out Will, which only fanned Katie's anger more.

"Isn't what it looks like?" Katie's voice went up an octave. "What am I supposed to think this is? Call me crazy, but I don't go flirting with my ex-boyfriends and claiming it's nothing. You see, I was raised to believe that words and actions meant something. Obviously, that's not true of either of you."

Will folded his arms and Katie knew she'd hit a nerve. Good. He deserved to be uncomfortable for the things he'd done. "That's not fair."

"Not fair? What's not fair is that I've poured everything I

have into building our relationship, yet somehow, that's still not enough for you."

"I was helping Megan work through some…issues."

Katie wanted to throw her hands up in the air but she kept them forced at her side. "What does that even mean? Issues?"

Will's eyes moved to Megan. "It's personal."

"Then maybe it shouldn't have had anything to do with you," Katie shot back.

"It's true, Katie," Megan tried again. "When he met me for lunch on Wednesday—"

Katie's eyes cut to Will and she could see the blood draining from his cheeks, leaving him pale. Stopping Megan with a swift movement of her hands, Katie repeated, "You went to lunch together on Wednesday?" Katie's voice thickened as all sorts of emotions lodged themselves in her throat. "And you didn't tell me? Why?"

Will shrugged weakly, his defenses falling the deeper Katie dug. "I was planning on telling you. I know it's not something I should have kept from you."

"Darn right it's not. I know I'm not a relationship expert, but if there's one thing I know, it's that couples have to base their relationship on trust and, already, you've proved that isn't a characteristic you value."

"I swear, I was going to tell you," Will insisted.

"Convenient. You were but I'm finding out now." Katie's anger threatened to bubble over and she covered her eyes with her hands, pressing her fingers into her temples to try and ward off the headache that was pressing in on her skull.

"Maybe I should go…" Megan looked away, holding one finger in her mouth as she nibbled on her manicured nails.

"No, don't bother," Katie said. "You've already won Will over. I can recognize when I've been beaten and I'd rather cut my losses now than keep letting myself get dragged through the mud."

"Katie. Don't." Will reached for her hand but she recoiled.

"No, you don't." She exhaled through clenched teeth, then chuckled darkly. "You know, until tonight, I've never felt like punching someone, but you've definitely gotten me the closest. If I weren't such a coward, I might ram my knuckles into your perfect jaw." A laugh mixed with a harsh scoff. "Apparently, Rex isn't the only guy who deserves it."

"Can we go somewhere to talk?" Will looked like he was about to drop to his knees and beg. It almost made Katie's resolve waiver, but she held steadfast, cemented there by her hurt feelings.

"No. There's nothing more to say."

"But there is," Will insisted. "I'm not ready to throw in the towel on us. We've only just begun."

Katie took a step back. "That's the thing about relationships. They aren't one-sided. You've done something that I don't know how I'll ever forgive and that's made me change my mind. No matter how much you want it, you can't have it. I have a say in all of this, too."

Will spoke softly and Katie was almost sure she saw his eyes go glassy with forming tears. "But I want you."

Katie's chin wobbled. She had to leave before she gave in. He had that kind of power over her and she resented him for it. It used to feel like she was bonded to Will; now, it made her a prisoner. She was going to escape while she still could. "Then you should have thought about that sooner."

"Katie." The heartache in Will's voice was real.

"It's fine. You're going to jet back to Austin and forget all about me and I'll move on. Eventually, I'll find someone who treats me with enough dignity to be honest. If I'm really lucky, he'll replace any memory of you."

"Don't say that," Will said softly.

Taking another step away to distance herself from him, Katie shook her head. "Ironic, isn't it?"

"What?" Will asked.

"It looks like I'll have to find a ride home for myself after all."

CHAPTER 14

Try as he might, Will couldn't get down the old farmhouse stairs without them creaking under every footfall. He cringed at the noise and held his breath until he reached the safety of the kitchen floor. At least there he could avoid the spots he knew would groan under his weight, and if he was lucky, he'd get out the back door and into his car without anyone being the wiser.

He needed time to think.

He needed to get out of Holly Wreath.

Lying in bed hadn't brought any relief in the form of sleep. Will's mind kept running over and over the same horrifying scenario at the social. The hurt and disgust on Katie's face kept flashing through his thoughts and he was sure he'd lost her for good. He'd done exactly what his family had warned him not to do and wouldn't blame them one bit if they cut him off and took Katie's side.

Any other morning, Will would have trotted down the stairs and met his parents for breakfast before starting his day, but they were still asleep. Before the sun was even considering lighting the horizon with its far-reaching rays,

Will had slipped on his clothes and shoved the clothes he'd brought back into his duffle bag, making sure to grab the keys to his rental car. He decided he was going back to Austin where he could let the dust settle and figure out what he was going to do. Staring at the ceiling, knowing Katie hated him and there was probably nothing he could do to convince her otherwise was going to make him go crazy if he stayed put.

He was frustrated and embarrassed, but pride kept him from confessing his feelings to anyone. Megan had offered to be a listening ear, but he'd pushed her away with clipped words and an angry glare. It wasn't all her fault, but she'd been a big part of it. If she'd talked to anyone else about her problems, none of this would have happened. Megan was hurt as she backed away, but Will didn't care. All he wanted was Katie. He wanted to be in her arms, running his fingers over her silky hair, kissing away her worries. If he showed up at her house, groveling on his knees, he doubted she'd even open the door for him.

His parents immediately knew something was wrong when he sat down at the table, his shoulders slumped in defeat. He'd tried to go after Katie, but she'd vanished. Charlotte tried to pry what had happened out of him but he kept his mouth clamped shut. There was no need to talk. It wasn't going to make a lick of difference.

"Trying to sneak out the door, are you?"

Will startled at the voice coming from the darkness. Grasping at the wall, he found the light switch with the help of the pale moonlight filtering in through the kitchen window. Blinking while his eyes adjusted, he found his father sitting at the table with a small box of glazed donuts sitting in front of him.

"Dad? What are you doing? Do you ever sleep?"

"Not when my son is making rash decisions." Roger's eyes

twinkled mischievously and he leaned back in his chair, putting his hands behind his head. With a smirk, he said, "I figured you'd try to do something stupid, like leave without saying goodbye."

Will huffed out a laugh. "Who said I'm going anywhere?"

"I kind of figured. That is your usual M.O. after all. The duffel bag gives it away, too."

"So? I don't want to sit around, feeling awful for what happened. Why's it a big deal if I go home to clear my head?"

"You say home like you mean Austin. That's not home. Holly Wreath is."

Will glared at the wall, directing his annoyance away from his father. His dad didn't deserve any of his rancor. "No, it's not. I'm back visiting. I've made my place in the world in Austin."

"Sit down, son. I think you've got enough time to have a donut before you run off and go and do something you'll regret."

Will eyed the donuts, his mouth watering as he tried to resist. His appetite had disappeared when Katie left, and now his stomach was angrily revolting. It wanted food. His father pushed the box closer, and Will's resolve failed. He reluctantly took a seat across the table.

"They're still warm," Will said as he pulled one from the box and licked his fingers.

"The best donuts in town are from the bakery before the glaze has even set. If you want something as sweet as these, you have to be willing to sacrifice to get it."

"Are you trying to get all deep and metaphorical, 'cause this seems like a comparison between donuts and Katie Holloway."

Roger expression was pleased and he shifted in his seat, adjusting the sling that kept his arm immobilized. "Or maybe a father merely wanted to share some delicious donuts with his son before he leaves for who knows how long."

Picking up the donut, Will took an enormous bite. It was the best donut he'd had in a long time, but it did nothing to cheer him up. He still had a black hole where his heart should have been and the donut might as well have been ash in his mouth.

Roger took a bite, licking the glaze from his lips. He pushed the box away from him. "I probably shouldn't have any more. I've already eaten three while I was waiting for you."

Will's feeble appetite disappeared. "You've been waiting for me?"

"Like I said. I was worried."

"You don't need to worry about me, Dad."

"I'm not. I'm concerned about Katie. Didn't I tell you not to mess it up with her?"

Will's eyes rolled like a moody teenager. Sitting back in his chair, he crossed his arms in front of his chest. "I wasn't *trying* to ruin it, but I did. I'm sorry I'm not perfect."

"Son, you're mistaking my intentions. I don't mean to be trapping you into anything."

"Then why does it feel like you're baiting me with donuts so you can catch me in order to give a lecture about how I've totally screwed up with Katie? Don't you think I know what a huge mistake I've made?"

Roger pushed the donuts further aside, like he was trying to get them out of his reach so he wouldn't be tempted to take another, and rested his good arm on the table. "Yes, I got the donuts to convince you to sit down for a minute with your old man, but I promise, I had no plan to lecture you. I think it's my duty as your father to make sure you're happy with your life, and if you're not, see if there's anything I can do to help you achieve the same level of happiness I've been blessed to have."

"Fine," Will sighed. "Fair enough. Impart your wisdom."

Will's dad stared at him, taking his sweet time before he spoke. "Did I ever tell you about how your mother and I met?"

"Yeah. You both grew up in Holly Wreath, were friends through school, got married and now, here you are."

Roger chuckled. "I think I might have given you the over-simplified version."

"From what I can tell, you and Mom have had smooth sailing for most of your life."

"Right." Roger laughed louder, holding up his bum arm. "This is the definition of easy."

Will's leg started bouncing. He'd already called for the jet to come to the nearest airport to pick him up. Wanting to throw himself back into work, he knew it would keep his mind off his misery. His dad was taking a little too long to get to his point, stopping him from escaping.

"No," Roger continued. "Your mother and I most certainly didn't start off on the right foot. I had the sweets for her, but was so shy that I couldn't hardly say two words to her. She was patient with me, but as saintly as she is, even her patience wore thin after a time."

"So what'd she do? It's not like she didn't end up with you."

Roger shook his head. "True. I have the advantage of hindsight, but at the time, it felt like my heart was torn straight down the center."

"What happened?"

"We were at our senior prom. I hadn't had the guts to ask her to go with me, so I made a plan to ask her when I found her there if she'd give me the honor of every single dance. There was just one problem."

"What?"

"She'd shown up with someone else. He was one of those sleazes who always made sure he had the prettiest girl on his arm, not because he wanted to spoil her, but because he knew it'd make him look good. When they arrived, it was all of ten minutes before I caught your mom's date making out with another girl over by the punch."

"What'd you do?"

"Nothing. I just stood there, frozen as an icicle. Your mom came over to say hello to me when she caught sight of her date with his arms around the other girl. Instead of defending her honor, or being a shoulder to cry on—anything would have been better than what I did—I did nothing. I watched your mother run away in tears, swearing off men."

"She obviously forgave you. I mean, it wasn't your fault the guy was a dirtbag."

"No, it wasn't, but it was my fault for being a coward. I was part of the reason she swore off dating for a time. It took me a solid six months of trying to win her over for her to even agree to go get a burger with me and even then, she insisted it wasn't a date. We were only going as friends."

Will put one leg up on his knee and ran his hand over the stubble that had started sprouting after he'd been clean-shaven for the social. "What has this got to do with Katie?"

"These kinds of delicate situations always boil down to the same basic problems. Lack of trust, being hurt when in a vulnerable situation, not being brave enough to fess up when a mistake has been made."

Will stared at the reindeer pattern of the tablecloth his mom had draped over the kitchen table. He'd definitely been guilty on all three counts of those particular transgressions.

"Katie's the best thing that's ever happened to me," Will said quietly.

RACHAEL ELIKER

"You can say that again. Your mother and I have been so pleased to see how happy you are. Both of you. The light is back in your eyes and you've been able to refocus on what's most important in life. Now, don't get me wrong. We're very proud of everything you've accomplished in your career, but that kind of success can come and go in an instant. Where you'll find the most joy is in the people you keep close to your heart and cherish."

"What am I supposed to do?" Will cleared his throat, forcing down the emotions that choked him. "I messed up big time."

"I don't need to know the details of anything, but first off, don't underestimate Katie. She's an absolute sweetheart and is stronger than she seems. Your mom, Charlotte, and I have watched her face tragedies with the kind of faith that makes the rest of us look like we're heathens. She'll come around."

"But I don't want to wait for her to decide to forgive me. It's killing me right now knowing she's probably still mad."

Roger nodded, brushing a few of his fallen crumbs off the table. "Some of it will take time, but I don't think you have to be idle. Once she knows you're penitent and truly sorry, you'll have to sweep her off her feet and remind her why she picked you in the first place because we all know, Katie's the type of girl who could have anyone she wants."

"Yeah, she is. Katie's so much more than my usual passing infatuation. She makes me feel...complete. Something is missing without her. It doesn't make sense, really. I've barely started getting to know her, but she feels so integral to my existence."

A chuckle rumbled from deep within Roger's chest, and Will smirked. He'd never been a romantic at heart, but Katie brought out all the mushy feelings. "You're like me, and we're both very practical men, but I'll be the first to tell you that love is anything but logical."

"So, you guys are all going to kick me out of the family if I can't win over Katie again?"

"I don't want to sway your decision, but yes. We all told you we'd pick her over you."

Will laughed, knowing his father was joking, but he knew they wouldn't stop inviting Katie over because he wasn't on good terms with her. "Win back Katie or end up an orphan."

Roger's grin widened. "Basically."

"No pressure then."

"Look. You're a man and have lived without us hounding you long enough, but I'll tell you this—in my experience, your mother has been a constant throughout my life. I'm not sure I could have done it without her, and if I did, I can tell you I wouldn't have had as nearly as satisfying a life as I've had so far."

Will mulled over his dad's words. "Katie is special, isn't she?"

"And be prepared to say goodbye to that every time you have to leave town."

"I know. That's been bothering me ever since I realized I liked Katie. It only intensified now that I'm sure I love her."

"Love is a strong word. Use it carefully."

"I am. I haven't ever said it unless I mean it."

"Good boy. I know you're painted as a heartbreaker sometimes, but I've always had a gut feeling that you're not using anybody in a way that would upset your mother or I."

"No, sir."

"Then the question you have to ask yourself is how are you going to win her back?"

"I don't know yet. I think I still have to figure it out."

Roger stood and walked around the table, clapping his good hand on Will's shoulder and giving him a firm squeeze. "Whatever you decide, your mother and I will be behind you all the way. Like I said, we want you to be happy, however that comes."

Nodding, Will let the conversation settle. Glancing at his watch, he stood and grabbed his duffle bag. "I'd better get going. I am heading back to Austin for a couple of days to get some things arranged with my company. I'll be back before Christmas."

"Have a safe flight, son. We'll keep your bedroom ready for you when you come back."

Will let himself out through the back mudroom door while his father tiptoed across the kitchen put the rest of the donuts in the breadbox. Shutting the door behind him, Will listened to the sound of his shoes crunching on another layer of freshly fallen snow. He thought about shoveling his parents' driveway for them before he left but knew he needed to catch his flight back to Austin as soon as it came in if he was going to finish what he'd planned to do. Besides, his gift to his father last year was an all-terrain utility vehicle with a snow blade on it and if there was one thing Will's dad enjoyed more than even mowing, it was bundling up and driving that thing around.

As Will unlocked his rental and tossed his duffle bag on the passenger side, a pair of blinding headlights came into view. Squinting against them, he could make out his sister's Porsche barreling up the drive. She skidded to a stop next to him and got out of her car, glaring at straight at him.

Will tried to tame her anger by joking, "You never were a morning person, but I see it's gotten worse with age."

Charlotte sneered. "I was hoping to catch you before you ran off, tucktailed like a scared stray dog."

"What, are you upset that I have to leave town and now you're going to be stuck cleaning Mom's chicken coop for her?" Will rested his arm on the top of his sedan, waiting for her reaction, although he was glad he had his car between him and his sister.

"No, it's you I'm ticked at."

"What a surprise. What'd I do this time?"

"You broke my best friend's heart!" Charlotte cried. Without warning, she bent over and grabbed a handful of snow, packed it together, and chucked it squarely at her brother with the kind of speed she'd honed as her softball team's pitcher. Will ducked as the snowball whizzed past, narrowly missing his face as it crashed into a pile of snow.

"Hey, watch it. You could give me a black eye as fast as you throw."

"What? You're worried you won't look pretty enough for your adoring fans?"

Will sighed through his teeth and pinched the bridge of his nose. "You're seriously going to give me grief for going back to Austin to make sure my company isn't going down the toilet while I'm gone? Because if I remember right, you never complain about the lavish gifts I bestow upon you for Christmas, all thanks to my job."

"You're not *that* good of a gift giver."

"I spent four hundred bucks on that set of haircutting shears for you!" He pointed to her car. "I won't even tell you how much of a dent that Porsche put in my savings. I bought it before I was a billionaire, you know."

"You can have all that stuff back." Charlotte paced the length of her car several times before throwing her hands up in the air and growling. "If you honestly are ready to give up a chance with Katie so easily, then you don't deserve her."

Will could feel the heat creeping up his neck, despite the temperature hovering below freezing. He wanted to refute his sister's punch below the belt, but he was more concerned with how Katie was doing than in maintaining any ego he might have left. "How is she?"

Charlotte stopped and planted her hands on her hips. "She was a sobbing mess when I swung by her house last night. The stupidest part of it all is that she's wondering if *she's* to blame for you being dumb."

"She's not," Will said softly.

"I know she's not," Charlotte huffed. "As long as I've known Katie, she's been determined to be buried in the same place she was born. You're the only one who's ever had enough sway to make her question her resolve. That's saying something. But you know what? Katie's strong. She'll get over you."

Will mirrored his sister's stance but dropped his eyes and toed at the snow. "I have to go."

"Of course you do. Go on then," Charlotte said, pointing her finger toward the horizon. "Nothing keeping you here."

Grabbing the door handle, Will hesitated opening it. "Tell Katie...tell her I love her and when I get back, I'm going to prove it."

CHAPTER 15

"Calm down, Katie." Katie blew a breath out through her lips and pinched her eyes closed. "No tears today. You have to focus."

She was surprised that her pep talk worked. The blurriness from her vision cleared and her heartbeat stopped thudding so hard against her ribs. After the social, she'd called a cab to take her home. Katie had managed not to cry until she could throw herself across her bed and scream into her pillows. It wasn't fair that any chance for happiness kept getting ripped away from her. Charlotte had stopped by and lent a sympathetic ear, but even seeing her was hard. Her eyes were the same color as Will's. After Charlotte left, Katie had fallen into a fitful sleep. When she woke up the next morning, she glanced in the mirror, aghast at her appearance. Her mascara had smudged and her hair was tangled in a way that made her look like she'd camped out under a bridge. Normally, Katie would have laughed but there wasn't even a spark of happiness left in her spirit.

She exhaled another breath and tried to keep her mind on happier things, like the fact that it was Christmas Eve and, with her efforts, she was going to make a lot of Holly Wreath residents have a merrier Christmas because they'd be able to share a home-cooked meal and some company when they otherwise would have been alone. Katie had even managed to arrange a white elephant gift exchange for people who wanted to participate. It was sure to bring a laugh or two, seeing what silly things people wrapped up. One year, she'd done one with the staff at the dental office and ended up walking away with a tub of cat litter. She'd never even had the desire to have a cat of her own, so she put it to good use and donated it to the humane society.

Without warning, her thoughts turned to Will. It wasn't fair that her mind kept betraying her when she was actively trying not to think of him.

He was supposed to be here helping her. He'd promised to be her sous chef, put up tables, decorate with red table-cloths and pinecone and holly stem centerpieces. But he wasn't there. Not that she'd expected him to show up after how the social had ended. He'd probably flown the coop and was back in Austin, enjoying the sunshine and warmer weather instead of the gray skies and snow that kept dumping on Holly Wreath. They were supposed to have another foot or so that night. Katie did her best not to think about the possibility of her car getting stuck in the snow on the way to the Christmas luncheon and how many people she'd disappoint if she was a no-show.

So much for happy thoughts.

She went ahead and let herself sulk. It had been days since the social and its aftermath still rattled her to the core. Maybe she'd been too hasty to judge. Maybe Will and Megan did have a good explanation for the precarious situation Katie had found them in. Misunderstandings had been known to happen. As much as she wanted to talk to Will and hear what was on his mind now that she had calmed down, she hadn't made the first move to contact him. She hadn't heard anything from him since she stormed out of the social either. Anything would have been reassuring and she would have gladly accepted his olive branch. But, there were no texts, no notes stuck under her windshield wiper, certainly no flowers.

To keep from going stir crazy, Katie had thrown herself into finalizing plans for the Christmas luncheon she'd been slaving over, trying to ensure it would be a success. In the end, the best location she could come up with to serve everybody was the church basement, and with the chairs and tables set up, it was going to be tight. People might even have to eat in shifts. She grinned to herself, though it was tinged with sadness. At least it would be cozy.

The additional stress of producing the meal she'd promised on a time constraint had turned her into a ball of nerves. She found herself at seven in the morning in the church's tiny basement kitchen, desperately trying to put together the feast she'd planned. The night before, she'd started baking pies from home and had made decent headway. Except when she skimmed over her to-do list, it looked like it hadn't been touched. There was still so much to do.

A swirl of cold air drifted down the stairs, and Katie's heart flopped in her chest. It was probably just the preacher coming in early to work on his sermon in his office. He knew she was going to be using the kitchen and had promised not to bother her. It was not Will. She had to keep herself from getting her hopes up, or she'd come crashing down from even higher heights. All that would do would hurt her more.

When she heard footsteps coming down the steps, she stopped smashing the diced potatoes she'd had simmering in a pot and listened. "Hello?"

"Katie? Are you down there?"

Katie's heart froze. What was Megan doing here? Katie

figured she'd gone back home to California, which would give Katie some measure of peace, knowing she'd never see her again. But no. Megan had to stick around and make sure Katie relived one of the worst days of her life, simply by showing her face again.

When Megan reached the bottom of the stairs, she kept her hand on the railing, warily watching Katie, like she was fully expecting Katie to give her another verbal lashing. Katie certainly thought about it.

Katie folded her arms, keeping the hurricane of emotions whirling in her under check. Her mother had always taught her to be civil and Katie could honor her in that way. "What are you doing here?"

Megan paused. "We need to talk."

A laugh tainted with acrimony came out, and Katie shook her head, going back to mashing the potatoes with renewed vigor. She knew she was being petty and immature, but as hard as she tried, her negative emotions were doing the driving. "I'm busy."

"I can see that. I promise I won't waste your time."

Her arm muscles burned as she continued to work on the mashed potatoes, taking out her frustrations on them, but Katie didn't quit. "Go ahead, I guess. Get whatever you need to off your conscience. I'm a good listener."

"So am I." Megan chuckled softly. "At least I like to think I am. Maybe that's another thing I've gotten wrong about myself."

Katie didn't say anything. She checked one of the turkeys she had thawing in the sink to see if it was going to be ready to roast Christmas morning. It was still solid and cold, so she drained the water to refill the sink with tepid water to speed up the defrost.

"Katie, first of all," Megan said softly, "I need to apologize."

Katie huffed and moved the frozen rolls from the counter to the table to give herself more space. "That's an understatement. Did Will put you up to this?"

"Will? No. I haven't seen him since he went after you at the social."

"Well, I didn't see him."

"Maybe he ran the opposite way as you. Trust me, he was desperate to find you and explain."

"Yeah? Where is he now?"

Megan looked away to the sacks of decorations Katie had left piled at the end of one of the folding tables. "From what I've heard, he's not in town."

Megan's words brought Katie to a screeching halt. That would explain a lot of things and it certainly confirmed Katie's suspicions. Will hadn't bothered to try and contact Katie because he'd cut his losses and skipped town. The realization hurt more than she wanted it to, but she kept her emotions locked up tightly. She'd become masterful at hiding her grief away from people when her mom was sick. Sure, she sometimes cracked, but usually, she could put on a brave face and keep people in the dark. It was easier that way. No looks of pity, no tears mirroring her own. She always felt so guilty when other people cried on her behalf.

"Then I guess he wasn't that desperate to see me after all."

"He must have had his reasons."

Katie shook her head, again tamping down the hope that kept trying to sprout. Will was gone. She'd had her chance, it didn't work out, end of story. "So you came to apologize out of the goodness of your heart?" Katie asked.

"That's right," Megan said. She straightened her shoulders proudly. "As hard as it may be to believe, I am trying to be a better person. Nobody else has to tell me how often I fall short and need to do better. My inner voice is harsher than any other critic I've had."

Katie stirred a stick of butter into the potatoes, watching it melt. "Alright. Fair enough. But if you are being honest, tell me what you and Will were talking about when I—" Katie wanted to say caught, but it seemed too accusatory and cruel, especially when Megan was trying to make things right— "found you and Will dancing."

Megan looked down at her shoes. "Will was giving me advice."

"About?"

Megan's cheeks burned red as hot coals. "About my boyfriend."

Katie had to repeat, making sure she'd heard her right. "You have a boyfriend? Then why on earth did you need Will?"

Megan squirmed under Katie's harsh glare. "I needed someone to talk to. Someone outside the situation so I could hear what I needed to without any sort of bias."

"Is your boyfriend breaking up with you?"

Megan shook her head. "No. Quite the opposite in fact. He asked me to marry him."

"Oh." Katie rolled her eyes as she went back to the potatoes. "You're one of those people who gets scared off when they find out someone else loves them. That must be hard, having so many people throw themselves at you."

Megan's expression drooped. "That's a little unfair, don't you think? I know my life may seem like it's been all sunshine, but I've had plenty of my own trials."

Thinking of her mother, Katie reined in her anger and apologized. "I'm sorry. That was unfair of me to assume."

"Apology accepted."

Grabbing a spatula from her pile of utensils, Katie scraped the sides of the pot and added a dash of salt to the mashed potatoes. "Why were you scared off by a proposal? I can't imagine your boyfriend is a loser."

"No, he's not. He's actually the sweetest guy I know and he complements me in a way I didn't know was possible." Megan smiled wistfully. "I don't know why, but it freaked me out. I started reviewing my entire life and was sure I was destined to break his heart. I don't want to hurt him. I didn't want to hurt you or Will. I don't want to hurt anybody, but I accept full responsibility that that's exactly what I did."

Katie's icy heart was thawing faster with Megan's help. Katie could tell Megan was penitent and doing her best to make it right. As much as the devil on Katie's shoulder wanted her to cling to her grudge, she never was very good at staying angry.

"I'll give you that's a difficult insecurity to overcome. Nobody knows the future and I'm not sure I'd want to invest in it if I was convinced it'd end in failure. I guess that's part of the risk we take in life. That we learn to love fully without fear." Katie glanced at Megan, who was looking down again and chewing her lower lip. "Tell me about your boyfriend. Is he cute?"

Megan looked up and her eyes brightened. "Yeah, he is. He's a different kind of handsome than Will, though. Blonde and lanky. He's a marathon runner. He's one of those genius types who doesn't mind being outwitted by someone else, including me, and he always makes sure to compliment me. From day one, all he's wanted was nothing more than to see to my happiness, even at the expense of his own."

"It sounds to me like you've worked out your own concerns. If he's willing to take you as you are, why shouldn't he be granted the same?"

A tear trickled down Megan's pink cheeks and she didn't bother to wipe it away. When she let out a breath, her whole body relaxed. An entire mountain of worry and regret seemed to be lifted from her shoulders.

"I think I need to give him a call and do some explaining,"

Megan said, "but first, I want to make sure you and I are okay. I know we were never friends in school, but I don't want to leave without you, knowing how sorry I am for this mess I brought you into."

Any anger Katie had felt toward Megan evaporated. Though Katie's emotions were still raw, she knew she was being honest when she spoke. "I forgive you. I'm sorry this hiccup happened, especially during the Christmas season when there should be peace and goodwill. I honestly do wish you all the best."

"Thank you," Megan said with more tears in her eyes. "I guess, Merry Christmas."

"Same to you. Have a safe trip home."

Megan nodded at Katie, starting up the stairs but stopping. "Can I help you? You look like you've got a lot to do."

Katie batted her hand at her observation. Not that it wasn't true, but keeping busy was keeping her sane. "I appreciate the offer, but if you're going to make it back to California before this snowstorm hits, you'd better get a move on it."

"Are you sure?"

"I'm sure it looks like chaos, but I promise I'm organized and have everything scheduled out. It'll get done."

Megan put her hands in her coat pocket and nodded. "Alright then. Maybe I'll see you around."

When Katie knew she was gone, she pulled out her phone and selected an upbeat Christmas playlist, making sure to put in her earbuds so she didn't disturb the preacher when he did come in for some quiet time to ponder and reflect on the scriptures as he prepared for the Christmas sermon. Katie danced and sang as she worked. Megan's apology had been refreshing and was enough for her to put aside thoughts of Will. The music was another dose of cheer that she needed to keep going. Even if Will called and confessed his undying love and she was able to find it in her heart to forgive him, he was still out of town. They would spend Christmas apart, which would mean it would be spent alone for Katie. There would be no makeup kisses or reassuring hugs. For all Katie knew, Will wasn't sorry for the way things had turned out.

Taking a package of pie crusts out of the fridge, she started working on the half dozen pumpkin pies she needed to check off her list when a hand clapped down on her shoulder. The touch startled her so much she shrieked and the cans of pumpkin puree in her hands went flying. Grabbing the rolling pin off the counter, she whipped around, ready to defend herself.

Holding up his hands and ready to surrender, the last person Katie expected to see grinning back at her was Will Ryan.

CHAPTER 16

"Will?" Katie looked like she'd seen a ghost. "What are you doing here?"

He knew it was a bold move but he reached over and pulled her earbuds out. It wasn't an accident that his fingertips brushed across her neck. He was glad that she didn't retract.

Will tucked his hands into the pockets of his jeans so he didn't immediately pull her into a hug. He wanted her to take the lead on how fast they'd move. If she wasn't ready to wrap her arms around him, then he would wait patiently until she was.

That didn't mean he wasn't going to try to convince her to forgive him with words.

"I'm here for you."

Katie studied his face momentarily before she slipped around him to pick up the cans she'd dropped. "I guess I assumed that. I don't think you would have snuck up on me if you were looking for someone else."

"I didn't mean to sneak. I thought you'd hear me coming down the steps. Sorry."

She set down the pumpkin and flicked her wrist at his apology. At the fridge, she pulled out a carton of eggs. "I guess I shouldn't have had the music so loud."

"I like hearing you sing and watching you dance. It's cute."

Katie's brown eyes cut over to him but she kept her expression masterfully guarded. He couldn't read her, so he didn't even try.

Katie continued to work as if he wasn't there, so he stepped back to give her space, watching her as she moved around the kitchen. For her age, she was very adept at cooking, a skill she'd probably picked up from her mother. Or maybe she'd acquired it when her mother got sick. It was another thing he didn't know about Katie that he wanted to find out. Ever since she'd left the social, he'd been kicking himself for letting their relationship get cut short because of his own stupidity. If he ruined it for good, he wasn't sure how he'd ever be able to move past the disappointment.

Setting down a large container of cinnamon, Katie braced herself against the counter and sighed heavily. "What are you really doing here, Will?"

The question hit him like a wrecking ball squarely in the chest. "I came for you."

"You said that."

"I wanted to apologize and let you know how badly I've missed you. Even if you never want to see me again, I still want you to know that I'm so sorry for how I've messed everything up. I fully accept my mistakes and am willing to accept any consequences for them."

Katie turned her back to him as she sifted through her collection of spices. "I forgive you."

Her words were simple and sounded sincere, but they left an apprehensive feeling in Will. "Would you do me a favor and turn around so I can look you in the face? I want to make sure you know my apology is sincere. You know my mom would insist the only way to properly say you're sorry is to be able to look the person in the eye."

Katie slowly faced him but closed herself off by folding her arms and tilting her chin up ever so slightly so she could watch him from the tip of her nose. "Alright. I'm listening."

Will's heart was beating in his chest faster than a hummingbird's wings. He knew what was at stake and he didn't want to mess it up more than he already had. Choosing his words carefully, he spoke. "First of all, I want you to know I take full responsibility for everything that's happened between us since the social. Before it, even. I wasn't totally honest with you and that wasn't fair."

The severity in Katie's gaze softened. When he looked deeply into her eyes, he was grateful she didn't look away. There was a chink in her defensive wall. "Go on."

"Of all people, I should know what a happy, stable, healthy relationship looks like. My parents have taught me from day one what it means to be committed and how to exist as equal partners. I should have come to you after I had lunch with Megan instead of hiding it. Actually, I should have told you I was having it in the first place."

"Yes, you should have," Katie said softly. "But I also don't want you thinking I'm controlling and jealous. I want you to help your friends when they need it. It's the hiding it that made me suspicious."

"Understandable. You can believe I won't be making that mistake again."

"I'd hope not."

Will let the conversation take a breather so Katie could absorb everything he was throwing at her. It had to be a lot to process and he wanted her to know he was sincere.

She was the first to speak again. "I thought you were out of town. At least that's what Megan told me."

"She was here?"

"Yeah. About ten minutes before you." Katie tilted her head. "I kind of thought you put her up to talking to me first."

Will shook his head and moved his hands to his waist. "I had no idea she was here and I wouldn't ask her to butter you up on my behalf."

"Good. Because that would have been a real turn-off, hiding behind someone else to do your dirty work."

"I'm not adverse to getting my hands dirty when it's required." Will grinned, but Katie looked away. It was still a little too early to use his charms. "What'd she say?"

"She was doing the same thing as you. Apologizing."

Will grunted, surprised by what Megan had done. "I hope she explained the situation."

"She did." Katie brushed her hands off on her apron. "Apparently I'm getting a bunch of apologies for Christmas."

A pang of sadness sliced through Will. "You deserve so much better than that. Neither of us should have treated you the way we did."

She gave him a one-shouldered shrug. "You were helping a friend and I can respect that. I was hurt by the fact that I was kept in the dark, but like you said, that'll never happen again, right?"

The way she kept a coy smile from curling her lips made Will's pulse quicken. There was the Katie he knew and loved.

"Was Megan right in telling me you'd skipped town?" Katie adjusted her ponytail behind her shoulder.

"I did leave, but I didn't skip town."

"Were you back in Austin?"

"Yeah. I had some things to get done at work, but now I'm back."

"You changed your mind?"

"Katie," he touched her cheek and she leaned into his hand, "I never intended on leaving permanently. There were a few things that needed my attention, but a lot of stuff I was able to put off until after the New Year. We do a company-wide shut down for the two weeks around Christmas and New Year's Day anyway, so people can spend time with their loved ones. Only a skeleton crew keeps working to troubleshoot for customers, but any big decisions about the company aren't going to happen while I'm here."

"Good. That's good." Katie's hands fidgeted like she wasn't quite sure she knew where to put them.

Will wasn't sure what else to say. He was so grateful that she'd forgiven him for his folly, but forgiveness didn't always mean things were instantaneously going to go back to the way they were.

He said the only thing that was on his mind. "Katie, I missed you so much."

Without even a thought of hesitation, Katie closed the gap between them and kissed him squarely on the mouth, igniting a fireworks display inside him. He staggered under the shock and she kept him from falling by grabbing fistfuls of his shirt until he steadied on his feet.

"You alright?" she asked with a pleased smirk.

Will's throat bobbed up and down. "Never better."

She drew him in for another fantastic kiss, and he lost all track of everything. His senses were heightened as he ran his hands over her bare arms and she tangled hers in his hair. When he pulled away, breathless and trembling, all he wanted to do was dive right back in.

"I'm so sorry, Katie. I swear I'm going to work every day from now on to make sure you never doubt me again."

Katie rested her head against his chest and she squeezed her arms around his waist hard enough that it made it hard to breathe. "I'm sorry, too."

"What have you got to be sorry for?"

"I could have given you the benefit of the doubt. It was

Rex who told me he'd seen you dancing with Megan, after all, and I know he did it to get me riled up. There's no way he didn't know what he was telling me would upset me, even if he was drunk and probably couldn't come up with a coherent thought otherwise."

"Rex was drunk at the social?"

"Slobbering. Very literally."

Will rolled his eyes. "Classy."

"Regardless, let's put this all behind us. We've apologized, gauged where we need to improve, and now I want to forget all about it."

"I can do that," Will murmured against her hair.

"I love you, so much."

Will's heart soared. "I love you, too. More than anything."

She moved her lips up to his and he relished another ardent kiss with her until he heard Charlotte choke out a cough from the stairs. "Okay, stop. I could have lived my whole life without seeing my brother kiss you like that, Katie."

Katie stepped back, simultaneously running a hand down her apron and one over her hair. He probably should have told her that her ponytail had been wrecked more than smoothing her hand over it could repair, but it was too cute seeing her frazzled.

"Charlotte? What are you doing here now?" Katie's eyes darted back and forth. "I didn't tell anyone I was going to be here this morning, yet everyone in the world has been able to find me."

"She has her sources," Will heckled. "She's a hairdresser, remember? Charlotte spends her days listening to old ladies gossip in her salon chair."

Charlotte moaned and rolled her eyes at her brother. "I do not only cut old ladies' hair. There are plenty of younger women who like to talk, too. The preacher's wife may have been in yesterday and let it slip that you'd be here."

"Okay," Katie said. "I need to be more tightlipped when I want to be alone, apparently."

"I still would have found you." Charlotte winked playfully at her friend.

"I'm sure you would." Katie took out her ponytail holder and combed her fingers through her hair. "That still doesn't explain why you're here. I didn't ask for your help with this luncheon until tomorrow morning."

"Didn't Will tell you?" Charlotte asked.

"Tell me what?" Katie glanced up at Will. "Are you keeping secrets from me again?"

"The good kind of secrets," Will said, lacing his fingers through hers. "Come on. We're here to help you pack all your stuff."

"My stuff?" Katie wasn't connecting the dots and Will didn't blame her. He'd purposefully been being sneaky because he wanted to see the surprise on her face when he revealed his plan to her.

"Yep." Will said. "As generous as it was of the church to let you have the luncheon here, it's not nearly big enough to fit everyone that's planning on coming."

Charlotte grabbed a couple of grocery sacks of decorations and started up the stairs. "Come on. Harvey's parking the truck and will be down to help. We're burning daylight!"

"She's right." Will's hand circled her wrist and tugged her along. "No time to waste."

"Where are we going exactly?" Katie grabbed her coat and slipped in her arms. She spun around the kitchen looking too frazzled to figure out where to start.

Will started packing up her spices. He leaned over to give her a quick peck on the cheek. "You'll see, but until we get there, it's a surprise."

CHAPTER 17

I t would have been almost too much if it wasn't so wonderful.

Will had made Katie promise to close her eyes as he helped her into his parents' machine shed. She obliged, covered her hands with her face, and stepped tentatively as he guided her with his hand on the small of her back.

"Alright." Katie could hear the smile in his voice. "Open your eyes."

Katie removed her hands and blinked a few times as she absorbed it all. Instead of tractors and a massive combine, the space had been cleared of all heavy machinery and every inch of the floor had been swept and scrubbed so thoroughly it looked clean enough to eat off of. There were half a dozen rows of fold-out tables, draped in white tablecloths—the real, linen kind, not the cheap plastic ones Katie had bought with her own money. The alternating red and green table runners were striking and Charlotte and Harvey were already arranging centerpieces on the tables, while Roger drug a couple more propane heaters at the far end to ensure the space would be toasty and warm as they worked. Even a

Christmas tree and a fake fireplace with three stockings hung above made a cozy-looking spot near the kitchen. The only thing that was missing was Santa in the velvet armchair.

"How did you...?" Katie's mouth fell open and she wasn't sure she'd be able to speak for the tears that were making her vocal cords seize up.

Will put his hands on her waist and brought her around to face him. "I was trying to figure out the best way to show you how much I love you and think that you're a magnificent person, then I remembered this luncheon. In a season where there's so much giving, you're the most generous person I know. You haven't stopped thinking about what other people need and striving to provide it. Finding a place to host it was the least I could do."

"It's incredible," Katie said, glancing over her shoulder once more to make sure she wasn't imagining things. "I can't wait to see everyone's faces tomorrow. This is really going above and beyond."

Will's smile was genuine, so much more than the polite stretching of his lips he tended to do when he appeared in public.

"Oh, no!" Katie slapped her hand to her forehead.

Will's hands were on her shoulders and he was ready to spring into action. "What is it?"

"There's only one problem." Katie chewed her lip. "I already told everyone who's RSVP'd that the luncheon would be at church."

"I've got you covered," Charlotte said as she hurried past with a glittering pair of reindeer to put on the table closest to the kitchen. "I swiped your list from your purse and already called everyone. They all know it's going to be here."

Katie's mouth gaped. "When did you do that?"

"When you stopped by the salon to go to lunch with me this past Tuesday," Charlotte said, looking rather smug.

"I can't believe you!" Katie cried with a laugh. "I thought you were acting strange."

"What was I supposed to do? You almost caught me like, three times. I had to tell you that you had lettuce stuck in your teeth to get you to go to the bathroom so I'd have a moment alone with your dang purse."

It felt so good to laugh. "Maybe next time, you should just ask."

"*Pfft*. And ruin the Christmas surprise? Don't be a Scrooge."

Will hugged her from behind and rocked her back and forth. Her heart, which had been so fragile and broken that morning, felt like it was stronger than ever before, mended together by so much love. It was incredible what forgiveness and understanding could do, and she was grateful she had been on the receiving end as much as she had given it to Will. They were flawed to be certain, but they were infinitely better together.

Leaning back against his chest, she closed her eyes, letting herself sink into the enjoyment of the moment. The strength and security of his arms, his masculine, musky cologne, his strong, steady heartbeat. Katie had never asked for much, but this was more than she could have ever hoped.

Carol came out of the kitchen with a festive apron tied around her waist to crack the whip. "Back to work, lovebirds. There's no time for snuggling right now."

"Yes, ma'am," Katie said, giving her a mock salute.

Will's mom pointed a ladle in Katie's direction. "For you, it's Carol."

"Right. Carol," Katie said.

"For him," Carol pointed straight at Will, "it's still ma'am."

Will followed Katie into the kitchen and he bumped into her when she stopped in the doorway. Carol's already impressive canning kitchen had been taken to the next level.

An extra oven, an industrial size fridge, and a deep freeze had been added sometime since Katie had helped her can apple jelly.

"When did this happen?" Katie asked.

"An early Christmas present from Will," Carol said as she stirred an enormous stockpot of food. "Maybe it was more for you than it was for me, though."

Will put his hands on Katie's shoulders and massaged them with his strong fingers. Katie had to clamp her jaw shut to keep from sighing with delight. "It's a multipurpose gift," he said.

"I can't tell you how much I appreciate this, Carol. Thank you for letting me use your fantastic kitchen, and for letting my guests invade your property."

"I'd hardly call it invading. So many of the people that are coming are my friends, too," Carol said. "I'm only sorry I didn't think of doing something like this for them sooner. I hate to think of anyone being lonesome for Christmas."

"Still, it's very generous of you." Katie glanced at Will, who'd slipped into the kitchen and was sneaking tastes of the soups his mother had prepared until she swatted him away with the ladle. Katie giggled as he picked up another serving spoon to try and defend himself. "I have a feeling this is going to go down in my personal history as one of my favorite Christmases ever."

When Will was bested by Carol in their mock-duel, he bowed at her superior serving utensil fencing abilities and went to the side of the fridge where he unhooked two aprons, tossing one at Katie.

She slipped it over her head and while she tied it around her waist, she looked down to read the scrawling lettering on the front. "Kiss the cook, huh?"

Will trotted over to her and put his hands around her, dipping her low while she squealed. "Don't mind if I do."

Despite his mother watching, Will kissed Katie in a way that made her knees go limp. She was totally under his control and, guessing by the devilishly charming grin he gave her when he pulled back, he knew exactly what he'd done. Good thing he was still hanging on to her or she'd be flat on her back.

Charlotte rushed into the kitchen. "Is everything alright? I thought I heard someone scream." Her eyes went to where Will was still cradling Katie. She touched her cheeks confirming that they were as hot as they felt, and produced a lopsided grin for her friend. Carol only laughed and shook her head, going back to babying her soups on the stove. "Oh. It's just you two. Again. Honestly, I can't believe your lips aren't constantly chapped for how much you kiss."

A nervous, self-conscious giggle made a sweat break out along Katie's hairline, but Will played it cool. He put Katie back on her feet and put an arm around her shoulder. "Let's just say I've had to buy lip balm in bulk lately."

Charlotte wrinkled her nose and pretended to get sick behind the door, then she disappeared back out into the seating area to continue pulling together the party's decorations.

"Who's on what job?" Carol asked. "I've got the soups covered, but today, we can get the turkeys and hams thawed, the rolls started, the Jell-o finished—"

Will was already at the fridge, taking out several quarts of heavy cream. "I'm making the sugar cream pies."

"Sugar cream pie?" Katie's imagination ran wild and she almost had to wipe drool from her mouth. "That sounds absolutely delectable."

"It's every bit as good as you're imagining." Will wiggled his eyebrows suggestively, making a burst of irreverent laughter rocket out of Katie.

"Is it your own creation?" she asked, gathering everything

she needed for the pumpkin pies she'd started at church but hadn't completed.

"I wish, but I'm not that clever. Not in the kitchen anyway. It's Indiana's state pie. I had it there last spring when I was there for March Madness and have tried a couple recipes to get it just the way I like it. Sweet, but not overly sugary, thick like a custard, but made without eggs. The nutmeg and cinnamon on top really sets off the flavor."

"Can't wait to have a slice," Katie said, cracking eggs into her own bowl.

Carol turned up the Christmas music she had playing from her wireless speaker and started singing along with *It's Beginning to Look a Lot Like Christmas*, and it wasn't long before Katie joined her. She danced while she worked and time seemed to fly by. They stopped for lunch when Harvey brought in sub sandwiches and drinks, but otherwise, were cooking and baking and making sure everything was just right for the morning. Harvey and Charlotte left for a dinner date they were having with friends and a few hours later, Carol dusted off her hands and wearily hung up her apron.

"I think I'm going to call it a day. The only other thing we have to do Christmas morning is get those turkeys in the roasting pans and bake the rolls. Otherwise, it's just setting things out." She shuffled to the door and Katie and Will followed as she turned out the lights. "Good night."

Carol tucked her hands between her arms and body to keep warm and Roger, who'd gone inside to fix them a simple dinner, came out to meet her with a blanket and a cup of hot chocolate. The sight made Katie smile and she wondered if, someday, that might be her and Will.

The promised Christmas Eve snowstorm had already started, and thick flakes of snow were drifting lazily from above, covering everything in white. It was the kind of

Christmas Katie preferred, even more so now that she had someone to snuggle up and share it with.

"I guess I'd better get going home," Katie said, staring at Carol and Roger's house as their Christmas lights twinkled against the darkness.

"Hang on," Will said. "Let's go get a bite to eat and relax. I'm not in any hurry to let you go again so soon."

"Alright," Katie agreed.

"One second." Will went back into his mom's canning kitchen while Katie waited outside, catching snowflakes on her tongue.

It took her a moment to realize Will had come back out and was staring at her. She shrugged against the feeling of discomfort. He wasn't saying anything. "What?"

"You are so beautiful."

She kicked her toe at the snow, blushing at his compliment. There wasn't anything she'd done in particular to try and make herself more alluring, and maybe that's why it felt all the more flattering. He never held back when he felt the need to say something kind.

"And you're charming and charismatic and absolutely, unquestionably a hottie," Kate said.

Will balanced a pie on his hand and walked over to scoop her up in his other. "I could easily think of a thousand more adjectives for you than you could ever possibly come up with for me, so be careful about getting into any competitions when it comes to saying nice things."

Katie playfully bumped him with her hip but conceded. Looking at his pie, she frowned. "You're not stealing a pie from the luncheon menu, are you?"

Tightening his grip around her, he kissed her snow-covered head. "Katie, darling, I counted, and there are no less than thirty pies in the fridge. Nobody is going to miss one. It can be our reward for a hard day's work."

"I can't argue with that."

Their feet crunched along the snow as they strolled to the house. Inside, the heat was welcoming and they kicked off their shoes in the mudroom entrance. Katie took the pie while Will hung up their coats. The light above the kitchen sink was on, but Carol and Roger had already gone up to bed, taking their dinner with them, leaving Will and Katie to themselves.

"Want to eat in the living room? We can turn on a Christmas movie and put our feet up if you'd like," Will offered.

"That sounds heavenly."

Will got out plates and utensils and heated up a leftover casserole dish of Carol's lasagna for their main course, though Katie was sure she wouldn't be able to wait much longer to try the sugar cream pie she was holding in her hand.

When they had everything they needed, Will led the way to the living room, setting down their dinner on the coffee table and slumping down onto the couch with a satisfied groan. The only light was coming from a modest Christmas tree glowing in the corner, but Katie liked it that way. It felt more intimate, like sitting next to a fire than having the room splashed with overhead lighting.

Will put his hands behind his head and locked his fingers. "I don't think I've worked that hard in a long time. It probably would have been easier to cater the whole meal, you know."

Katie sat next to him and poked him in the side hard enough to make him yelp and sit up defensively, waiting for her to start a tickle attack. "I know that, but there's something special about sacrificing for others. Plus, the food will taste a million times better than if it's reheated and reconstituted caterer food."

"Yeah, that's true." Will sat forward and grabbed the pie with a couple of forks. "Here. Try a bite."

"You're not going to cut a slice?"

Will laughed at her. "You're so naïve. Once you take your first bite, you're going to thank me for not limiting you to a single slice."

He offered her the first bite, spearing a large piece from the very center and bringing the fork to her mouth. She ate it, and in an instant, she was converted. The sugar cream pie was everything she'd imagined it would be.

"Oh, wow," she said around a mouthful of pie. "That's incredible."

"Told you." Will took an enormous bite and grinned at her, reaching over to wipe her lips. "Whoops. Looks like I missed and got some on your face."

After eating half the pie, Katie had to put it down, not because she didn't want more, but because she knew she'd keep eating until she had a stomach ache. Will turned on the big screen television mounted above the gas insert fireplace and made sure the fire was going below to set the ambiance. It was such a simple, unassuming way to spend the evening, but it was so romantic that Katie knew she'd choose a quiet night with Will like this over a fancy ball where she'd get to dress like a princess any day.

Close to midnight, Katie had to start fighting to keep her eyelids from drooping shut. The early morning, long day, and intense emotion, all coupled with a full belly made it impossible to ward off sleep. It didn't help that Will had taken off her socks and was rubbing her heels. More than once, she mentioned that he missed his calling as a masseuse.

"Katie? Are you asleep?"

"No." She sat up and leaned against Will's arm, gripping his hand between hers. "I should be though. Santa can't come if we're being naughty staying up late and trying to catch a glimpse of him."

"Funny you should mention Santa, because I have a favor to ask of you that involves Old Saint Nick."

Katie's resolve to keep her eyelids from fluttering shut was abandoned and she let out a hearty sigh. "I'm listening."

"Someone asked me a favor and I said yes."

"Who asked?"

"Rudger Pierce."

"Who?"

"Piper Woodhull's new guy, remember? He said he met you at the parade."

Katie's brain was sluggish with sleep, but eventually, she remembered his face. "Right. Yeah. I remember him. What did he want?"

"He hurt his shoulder doing some ranching and, at the social, he asked if I'd be able to help him out with something he'd been planning on doing."

"He needs you to play Santa for him?"

Will delicately brushed his fingertips down her cheek and smoothed them over her head, making her shiver with delight. "Sorta. He had planned on playing Secret Santa to the kids around town who aren't so fortunate. I agreed."

"Good thing you have a Santa suit already." Katie yawned. "You were definitely the most handsome Santa I've ever laid eyes on."

"I'm flattered." Will's chuckle shook Katie, but it did little to rouse her. "I was wondering something though."

"What's that?"

"I wanted to know if you'd be the Mrs. Claus to my Santa again."

Even as she was drifting off to sleep, she smiled, remembering how much fun the kids had during the parade seeing her and Will dressed up as Santa and Mrs. Claus. "I'll always be your Mrs. Claus."

"Good. I hope you don't mind, I had Charlotte go over to your place and she used the spare key under your flowerpot to pick up your costume a couple days ago and I sent it out to the dry cleaners."

Katie shrugged lazily. "Perfectly fine with me. When do I need to meet you to deliver presents?"

"Early. We don't want any children spying on us when they should be in their beds."

Katie's closed her eyes for good and she curled her legs up under her on the couch. "Then we'd better get some sleep."

Will shifted under her and a moment later, she felt a soft blanket being arranged over her. "Thank you," she murmured.

A clock somewhere in the house chimed midnight. Pressing a kiss to her temple, Will whispered, "Merry Christmas, Katie."

"Merry Christmas to you, too." Reaching her arm around his waist, she snuggled in closer to him. "Thank you for making this year the best one yet."

CHAPTER 18

Even with gloves on, Will's fingers were beginning to feel like they were turning into popsicles. They'd finished their first stop at Piper Woodhull's house, covertly shoveled her driveway, and left a gift on her front porch without waking her.

Katie climbed in on the other side of the truck and shut the door, blowing her breath across her fingers to warm them up. "What do you think's in the box Rudger had us leave for her?"

Will started the truck, cringing at how loud it was. He hurried to put it into drive so they could leave the scene of their charitable service and move onto the next person on their list. "No clue. Whatever it is, I'm sure Piper's going to love it."

"I hope so. She's one of those amazing people that deserves all the happiness in the world."

Cranking up the heat, Will put his hand over Katie's. "So do you."

Just like the first time she'd donned the outfit, Katie made Mrs. Claus look fantastic. They'd fallen asleep on his parents' couch and though it left him with a crick in his neck, he didn't mind one bit. Waking up to Katie was the best Christmas gift he could have wished for.

"The next stop is a block ahead." Katie tossed the paper Rudger had given them up on the dash. Looking around the cab of the truck, she asked, "Why did you have to borrow Rudger's truck, anyway? You bought your parents that nice one. Wouldn't that work?"

"Apparently, it has a tendency to get stuck in the snow, which my father found out when he tried to drive it to town to pick up a gift for my mom. Rudger's truck is a little more manly and can get the job done without any trouble."

"So, their truck has a bum door and can't handle snowy roads?"

"Basically, yep."

"Good call then. I'd hate to be stuck on the side of the road in this snow."

"I wouldn't think it was all that bad if I was with you. I'm sure we could find plenty of ways to stay warm." Will moved his eyebrows in a way that made Katie laugh and smack his shoulder.

"Don't you forget, I'm a lady."

Pulling alongside the curb a few houses away from where they were to make their delivery, he leaned over and kissed her cheek. "I'd never forget, though that doesn't mean I don't think you're tantalizing."

She accepted his praise with a gentle smile. Pushing open her door, she made sure to close it as quietly as possible. Every noise seemed to be amplified by the cold. Will hopped into the bed of the truck and found the sack of gifts for the household. Accepting it with open arms, Katie carried it to a beautiful brick home with white trim and black shutters. Stopping in the middle of the street, she looked up.

Will leaped out of the truck and jogged to catch up with

her. Putting his hand on the small of her back, he followed her line of sight to see what she was staring at. Seeing nothing, he tried to coax her forward. "If we don't hurry a little, we're going to freeze right here."

Katie's breath curled into wisps as she spoke. "I want to take it in, that's all."

Will nodded, realizing he wasn't truly savoring the experience in his rush. "I guess I've become so used to living in a larger city that it takes a lot to compare to a big city skyline. There's not much that can outdo being surrounded by the twinkling lights of skyscrapers."

"A big city skyline?" Katie snorted. "Please. Are we looking at the same pre-dawn starry sky or not?"

Will tipped his head back and looked again. The shine of infinite stars that filled every inch of the sky stirred something within him. He couldn't remember the last time he'd slowed down enough to appreciate them.

"No skyscrapers to block the view, no traffic to disrupt the silence," Katie said with pride. "Please don't tell me you prefer artificial city lights to the kind of majesty the universe can provide."

"You got me there." Will stood beside her and watched the stars twinkle and it filled him with wonder. If they were lucky, they'd get done before the sun rose and would get to watch it together as they drove back to the Ryan's farm. The sunrise was Will's favorite part of the day and it seemed fitting to be able to share it with Katie. He looked over at her, the contours of her face lit by the soft glow of nearby Christmas lights. "I don't know how you do it."

"Do what?"

"Live with this kind of zest for life. I can't even remember the last time I even gave the stars a passing glance."

She pat him on his overstuffed Santa belly. "You've got a

talent for the kind of hard work that requires you to always be on the go, but maybe this can serve as a reminder that it's important to slow down once in a while and appreciate the journey you're on."

A laugh slipped from Will's throat and he hugged Katie closer to himself. "There you go again, imparting your particular brand of wisdom. I will take your advice, though, especially if you're there to slow down with me."

He sealed his promise with a kiss and they continued on their mission, dropping off a bag of several gifts on the front step. Will had no idea who lived in the brick home, the hardship they were going through, or how Rudger found out about them, but he felt honored to be part of the process that would undoubtedly bring a measure of happiness to the home.

Back in the truck, they drove a few blocks down and swung a right, parking several houses away from their destination so they wouldn't make it too obvious what they were up to.

Katie was reading through the list, committing to memory everything that needed to be retrieved from the truck bed. Will's insides quivered with nervous energy and he was excited but apprehensive to give her his Christmas present. It wasn't tangible or lavish, but he had a feeling she wouldn't mind.

"Ready?" Katie asked, her eyes alight with eagerness.

"First, I wanted to give you my Christmas present."

She wrinkled her nose and Will loved the way it tugged the freckles across her nose. "Don't you want to wait until we're with your parents after the luncheon? We were all going to open gifts then."

"I know, but I'd rather do one of mine now, while we have a moment alone."

Katie's face shifted with curiosity, but she did her best to remain patient. "Alright. Hand it over, Santa."

Will shook his head and pulled down the fake beard that had been itching his face. "It's not something you can hold. Not unless you count holding me, I suppose."

Katie's confusion only grew at his cryptic answer. "Is this some kind of riddle I have to solve? Because I'm telling you right now, I'm going to smash it. I can do crosswords like a boss, thanks to my mother. Any riddle you might give me will be a piece of cake."

Chuckling, Will shook his head. "I'm not that clever. This one, I'm going to give to you straight."

"Alight." Katie folded her hands in her lap. "Hand it over."

Pushing aside the doubt that his gift wouldn't be well-received, he took a deep breath to help build the anticipation.

Instead of a lengthy monologue, explaining his motivations and hopes, he simply said, "I'm back."

It took a second for it to register, but when it did, Katie's eyebrows went up. "Back temporarily or back for good?"

Will's smile crept up his lips. "Back for good."

"How?" Katie closed her eyelids, then opened them and looked straight at him. Straight into his soul with her intense, glittering eyes. "Your company is in Austin. They need you there."

He shook his head. "Remember how I told you I'm more the face of the company than anything?"

"Yeah."

"That means I don't need to be at the office every day, troubleshooting technical issues. Besides, part of the beauty of technology-based companies is that so much of it can be done remotely. Sure, I'll have to travel a couple of times a month for press conferences and events, but you already promised you'd go with me."

Moving loose hair from off her face, Will could see her

hands were trembling. "You're moving back to Holly Wreath?"

He nodded. "I've already been talking to a contractor about building a house. My parents have graciously given me ten acres of their property. I had the surveyor out this past Monday."

"They'll love having you live next door." The joy he was hoping his confession would bring had begun spreading across her face until she was smiling all the way up to her eyes.

Will chuckled softly. "Next door is a relative term. The land they gave me is a mile down the road on the opposite end of where they live."

Katie laughed. "That sounds like your parents. Not wanting you to drive them crazy by being too close."

Scooting closer, Will reached for Katie's hands and she delicately placed them in his. Words couldn't describe how wonderful it was to feel her touch. Every single time, it sent a jolt of excitement that was energizing and made him feel that there wasn't anything he couldn't conquer. "As much as I love my family, they're not the reason I'm coming back to Holly Wreath."

Katie averted her eyes. "Please don't say it was all for me."

Bringing her chin up with his finger, he coaxed her gaze back to his. "I have absolutely no problem saying this is because of you."

"Why?"

"I..." Will tried to get his brain and mouth on the same page. "Ever since I first saw you in the diner, I was reminded there was something exceptional about you. I couldn't quite put a finger on it, whether it's your infectious, stunning smile, or the way your eyes dance with excitement as you talk about things you're passionate about. Maybe it's your simple, joyful approach to life in general. Whatever it is, I haven't been as happy as I am with you in a long time. Maybe ever."

"So, you're not basing your decision to move back because I'm an excellent kisser, are you?"

Will's laugh came from deep within. "I'm not going to lie and say I haven't been enjoying your expert kissing skills."

Reaching around the back of his neck, she tugged him in for a kiss. There was a hunger behind it that sucked Will in and made him never want to leave. He loved feeling connected with her in a way that words could never adequately express. He didn't want their kiss to end.

Then the driver's door was yanked open.

Katie squealed at the intrusion and Will pulled his beard back up to mask his identity. Shifting his attention to the open door, he recognized Piper Woodhull staring at him with intense confusion.

She was in her pajamas, holding an open box with a fancy pair of cowgirl boots inside. A basset hound wagged his tail behind her as his tongue lolled out the side of his loose jowls. Piper must have spotted them while they had delivered her gift and suddenly, Will felt antsy to get going. If she saw them, that might mean the rest of their delivery route would, too.

Will was a silent listener for the most part, while Katie did the talking. Piper had a look of desperation to her, but there was still hope in her eyes. Rumor—which he'd gotten straight from Charlotte—was that she'd hit a rough patch with Rudger. It made sense that she had been their special stop along the gift delivery route. As little as he knew Rudger, he could tell he was a decent guy and Will knew just as well as anyone that sometimes, even guys with a good heart could make mistakes. He hoped things worked out for Piper and Rudger. They seemed like the kind of couple that reminded him of his parents. The kind of couple who could be enduring.

That's what Will had dared hope for Katie and him.

When Piper left, shutting Will's door, he watched her jog back home in his rearview mirror.

"I guess we'd better get moving," Will said, reaching for the door.

"Hold on a second." Katie grabbed a handful of his fluffy white collar and yanked him over, stopping with his face mere inches from hers. "I wasn't done kissing you."

He indulged her in another fantastic kiss that left him totally weak and at her mercy. When she sat back, a goofy, delightful grin stretching her lips, he quipped, "Okay, I lied. I'm totally moving back because you're such a great kisser."

Katie giggled and stepped out of the truck, reaching in the back for the needed gifts. Meeting her on the other side, he enveloped her in a hug, guiding her head to his chest and running his fingers along the soft skin under her ear.

"Now who's going to make us late?" Katie murmured against his chest.

"At least no one would be surprised to see Santa and Mrs. Claus kissing, don't you think?"

Bending down, Will gave her one final kiss. Though it was pure and innocent, it was just as powerful as the one they'd shared in the truck. Will loved that about Katie. No matter how she gave of herself, it had the power to stir his soul in a way he had never known.

"I feel bad," Katie said.

"Why's that?"

Her shoulders shrugged. "I didn't bring anything to give to you. I'm getting a one-sided Christmas gift and it's making me feel guilty."

Will gently put his hands on her cheeks and brought her eyes up to meet his. "Maybe I feel spoiled and selfish because you already have given me the best Christmas gift I could have imagined."

Her right eyebrow inched up in question. "And what's that?"

"Your love."

CHAPTER 19

"I can't believe we've pulled this all off," Katie said as she stacked hot, buttery rolls into dozens of baskets. The Ryans had provided enough that each table would have two of their own.

Will poked his head out of the refrigerator, where he'd been pulling out all the cold food items—pickle trays, deviled eggs, Jell-o, and enough whipped topping to sink a ship. "You mean that we delivered all the presents on time?"

"That and that we didn't get caught."

"There were a couple of close calls." His crooked grin was so cute. "That loudmouthed beagle at the trailer park nearly gave us away."

Katie tipped her head back and laughed, remembering how Will barely outran the dog back to the truck. It wouldn't have been able to do much damage for its size, but the beagle was determined to sink his teeth into Will's ankle.

Will must have been replaying it in his mind, too. "I would have been limping for weeks if that dog got me. He was small but his teeth were sharp."

"I think your imagination is remembering the dog as more vicious than it was."

"I could see the glint of his teeth. It was definitely a rabid monster after me. He could have chewed my foot right off, then I'd be bedridden for days. Weeks, maybe."

"I don't know of many people who would complain of a reason to have to sit around with their feet up," Katie teased. "I'd wait on you hand and foot until you recovered."

"Maybe I should have run slower." Katie scrunched her face and chucked a roll at him. Instead of ducking and letting it fly past, he caught it and took a bite. "Thanks."

"You looked like you were struggling a bit. I've been telling you that you need to get your personal trainer to write up a cardio workout for you, too. Never know when it'll come in handy."

"Okay, first of all, I was only winded because I had to run with an enormous fat Santa suit on. I might as well have been running with sacks of potatoes on my shoulders."

"Uh, huh," Katie teased.

Will took out the olives and stuck out his tongue, seeing the black ones had been arranged next to the green ones. "You want me to go ahead and toss the green ones in the trash? That's what's going to happen at the end of the day when nobody eats them."

"I'll eat them if no one else does because they're delicious."

Before Will could offer another rebuttal, the kitchen door swung open. Carol, Charlotte, and Delores Stanley bustled into the kitchen.

"Merry Christmas, Delores," Katie said. "I'm so glad to see you. How've you been?"

Delores smiled at her. "Oh, wonderful, dear. I see you've been busy, too." Her glittering eyes flashed over to Will and her smile increased, threatening to split her face.

Katie pretended she didn't notice her implication. "Getting this luncheon ready has been my baby for most of December. It's taken up a good portion of my free time."

"Well, we appreciate it. It's been entirely too long since Lester and I have enjoyed a feast like this. I can't seem to muster up the resolve to do the cooking myself. My old bones are too tired and my son never picked up any skills in the kitchen. I hope you don't mind, but we brought Timothy with us since his dad is clearing roads this afternoon."

Katie reached across the island and took Delores' hand. "First of all, it's my privilege to do the work for you. And of course, Timothy is welcome. Today, I want you to sit back and enjoy yourself."

"I will, once I help get everything set out. I don't mind being a server." Delores grinned again. "That's the easy part."

"I certainly appreciate it," Katie said. "Can I say you look wonderful, too? Your dress is so festive and your pearls set off your beautiful white hair. You're the embodiment of Christmas cheer."

Leaning in close, Mrs. Stanley whispered, "The secret is the blue shampoo. Charlotte always does such a good job keeping my white hair from yellowing."

"Charlotte?" Katie said. "You don't do the blue shampoo at home?"

Mrs. Stanley pointed to herself and shook her head. "Me? Oh, no. I'm not going to mess with that stuff. I'm not about to dye my head blue because I've done it wrong. I'm not hip enough to have hair that's any color of the rainbow."

"I see," Katie said as her eyes wandered around the counter until she was next to her friend, who was watching them talk with wide eyes and a subdued grin. "That's very interesting. Did you hear her, Charlotte? She said she never messes with blue shampoo because she's afraid it'll dye her hair. Delores said she always has you do it for her."

"Yeah. It's a trick of the trade," Charlotte said with an expression that betrayed her guilt. "What are you trying to insinuate?"

"I think you know what. When you were supposed to go pick up donations with me, you called and backed out because you said Delores was having a hair crisis. She just told me that *you* do her blue shampoo for her because she's terrified of ruining her hair."

Charlotte's mouth gaped open and shut before she spit out, "So?"

"So, I think you were meddling in my love life and trying to set up Will and me."

"And?"

"And didn't you promise you wouldn't?"

Charlotte's face drained of color. Pointing an accusatory finger at Carol, she cried, "My mom was in on it, too! She texted me and told me when to call!"

Carol shrugged, indifferent to Charlotte shoving the blame in her direction. Will leaned against the counter, folding his arms and unwittingly showing off the veins and muscles of his forearms, where he'd rolled up his sleeves. The sight may have distracted Katie momentarily.

"So what if I did?" Carol said smugly. "I only mess with affairs of the heart when I know it's going to be a win."

Carol held up her hand for Charlotte to high five and her daughter smacked her palm against her mother's.

"Yeah, I'm not sorry," Charlotte said, playing off Carol's coolness. "I had a hunch a long time ago that you were drooling over my brother and when we saw the opportunity to help out, we didn't hesitate."

Katie glanced at Will, who shrugged. "Don't look at me. I had no idea they were setting us up. Not that I'm going to complain. It might have taken me longer than I would have liked to work up the courage to ask you out if they hadn't."

"Isn't that sweet?" Delores wiped a tear from the corner of her eye. "Young love. What a blessing."

Carol clapped her hands and rubbed them together. "As much as I love seeing how my children have found happiness, there are a lot of hungry people out there that want to eat. Let's not keep them waiting."

Delores and Charlotte both took two baskets of bread each, while Carol stacked up as many pies as she could handle. Katie was about to take a couple of the deviled egg trays when Will caught her by the belt loop of her jeans and tugged her back to him.

"Hey!" she cried. "You about made me spill."

"Oops. Sorry." He put his hands on her hips and spun her around, keeping his hands where they were. "Not."

"Don't tell me. You hate deviled eggs, too." He didn't speak, only studying her face, his eyes eventually leading back up to hers. "What?"

"I was just thinking."

"About?"

"You." He kissed her once, generously but far too brief for her liking.

Katie glanced back at the door. "We're going to get caught smooching again if you're not careful. I don't know about you, but it's a little embarrassing how many people have walked in on us."

Will kissed her again and whispered in her ear, "I don't care one bit that they know I'm hopelessly smitten with you."

A giggle bubbled out of her. Katie thought she'd never get tired of hearing him say that to her. She'd waited so long to be the focus of his affection and, now that she had it, she never wanted to be without it again.

"You know, I suspected my mom and sister all along." A suave smirk graced his lips.

"Did you?"

"Yep. And why would I want to stop them? I was looking for a chance to take you out and they made it all too easy." Will let go of her and picked up the biggest platter, stacked full of sliced ham.

"Well, then I guess I shouldn't have been worried about them and their meddling. I just didn't want a pity date from you. That would have been worse than you ignoring me altogether."

"Think we should forgive them?"

Katie nodded curtly. "I think I'll get over them not being able to mind their own business."

Katie nudged the swinging kitchen door open with her foot and stepped out into the main section of the machine shed, except it hardly looked like it was a building for storing tractors. Charlotte, Roger, and Harvey had outdone themselves. The decorations were stylish and screamed Christmas and the entire area was cozy and warm thanks to the propane heaters. Almost every seat at the tables had been claimed and a teary smile emerged from Katie when she looked around, recognizing so many faces from around Holly Wreath. She knew acutely how hard it was to be alone during the holidays and was so grateful for the opportunity to serve them at the luncheon. Being there was just as important to her, too.

A big portion of that gratitude had to go to Will. Without his help, there was no way it could have been so successful. His compassion and love had filled an empty space inside her that she'd been longing to overcome, but had never been able to quite do on her own. They were a good team.

Timothy was sitting next to Lester. When Timothy spotted Katie walking by, he smiled and waved her over. Will continued on to set down the ham while Katie veered off course to say hello.

Katie grinned at the teenager. He'd tried to tame his wiry

hair by parting it and had on an ugly but very festive sweater, complete with bells sewn onto the front that tinkled every time he moved. "Merry Christmas, Timothy."

"Merry Christmas," he replied. "Thanks for putting this together. My grandparents have been looking forward to it all month."

"I'm honored to have all of you here with us."

"Thanks." Timothy glanced at his grandpa, who was talking to another elderly gentleman across the table. Waving Katie closer, she leaned over to hear what secret Timothy had to share. "I wanted to say I'm sorry it didn't work out."

As fast as Katie's mind could race, she had no idea what he was talking about. "Huh?"

"About going together to the Christmas social. My grandpa mentioned that you'd make a good date, but he didn't know I already have a girlfriend."

Katie almost couldn't stop a snorting giggle. Almost. He was being so sincere that she knew it would hurt his feelings if she laughed in his face. Masterfully, she kept her expression neutral and nodded. "Yes, I remember you mentioning your girlfriend when you were in for your last dental cleaning."

"I did? Oh, that's right. Yeah. I forget who I've already told. She's my first one, so I might be a little obnoxious about it."

"Understandable. I'm glad it worked out for both of us."

"Me, too. It's pretty awesome you're dating Will. He's cool."

"He is. And I'd love to meet your girlfriend sometime. Maybe we can all go on a double date sometime. Bowling or something."

Timothy nodded and Katie excused herself to put the eggs down on the serving table. The rest of the food was being brought out by Harvey and Will and seeing it all set down, Katie felt a swell of pride for all their hard work. Having missed breakfast in the busyness of the morning, her mouth watered, ready for lunch herself. She hoped there was a slice of sugar cream pie with her name on it.

With the food set out, Katie sought out Roger and asked if he'd offer a prayer so they could get to eating.

"Anything you ask, Katie," he said, patting her shoulder. Raising his booming voice, it echoed in the spacious room. "Folks, if you don't mind, we're going to say a prayer of thanks so we can get started eating."

She went back to Will, who wrapped his arms around her from behind and rested his chin on her shoulder. Brushing her hair out of the way, it made her skin tingle. She bowed her head and closed her eyes, but didn't even try to resist a smile.

Taking his cap off his head, Roger bowed his head as everyone else followed suit, reverently listening to his prayer. Roger spoke eloquently and respectfully, as if it was a friend listening. He thanked the Lord for Katie's efforts, for the season to celebrate the Savior's birth, and for the bounty they had before them. Peeking through her eyelashes, Katie peered around. There were people there she'd known her whole life, and though her family was gone, she wasn't alone. Wrapped in Will's arms, she felt like she had a family again.

At the conclusion of the prayer, Carol turned on the music for background ambiance and conversation filled the air. The entire day was a blur. Katie made sure to keep the food stocked until it started running out. Her feet were tired and her back was getting sore from all the heavy lifting, but she didn't mind. The happiness she saw on each and every person's face was worth it.

Will made sure she took time to eat. Instead of sitting at the tables, he lured her back to the kitchen, where they sat on the counters, swinging their legs and commenting on how delectable all the food was. Katie made sure to nab another slice of Will's sugar cream pie before it was gone. She was going to have to run a few extra miles on her treadmill to offset the meal, but every bite was worth it.

The sun was starting to sink lower in the sky by the time they said goodbye to their last guest. The white elephant gift exchange was every bit as entertaining as Katie had hoped. The Stanleys walked away with a bag of dog food for a dog they didn't have, another couple took home a grilled cheese toaster, and Katie earned herself a container of beard balm. When Will teased her about it, she shrugged, said it smelled nice, and that she'd always wondered what he looked like with a beard.

Thankfully, Will also had the foresight to buy carryout trays in bulk, so they could send home the leftovers with people rather than trying to figure out what to do with the extra food, not that there was much left by the time they were finished. Ready to get to tackle the dishes and clean up the kitchen, Carol shook her head and pushed Katie out, shutting off the lights.

"If there's one thing I've learned, it's that dishes are patient. They'll still be dirty tomorrow."

"Besides," Will said, holding her hand as they walked to the house, "Santa visited and we still have presents to open."

Katie stared at him. "You had time to shop?"

"No, Santa delivered them," Will insisted.

Charlotte snorted. "Right. If by Santa you mean personal assistant."

"I may have had her shop for you, but I'll have you know I did all of Katie's myself," Will said proudly.

"All?" Katie repeated. "Please don't tell me you went crazy and bought me a thousand gifts."

"A thousand? No." Will shook his head. Katie reached

over and pushed aside some of his hair. "It's closer to nine hundred and ninety-nine."

"Great. I only got you one," Katie said, covering her eyes with her hand. "I wasn't even sure I was going to be able to give it to you."

Will tightened his grip on her hand. "I'm going to love it, no questions asked."

The Ryans, Katie, and Harvey gathered inside. Charlotte relaxed in the recliner and Harvey sat at her feet, grinning the entire time as she played with his hair. Katie and Will sat at one end of the couch, snuggled together while Carol and Roger held hands at the other.

The tree was loaded with gifts and Katie quickly discovered Will wasn't kidding about the gifts he had bought to lavish on her. By the time she opened up a pearl necklace, she grinned sheepishly at him, insisting it was all too much. He insisted it wasn't.

Charlotte and Harvey left around seven to celebrate Christmas with his sister and her family. An hour later, Carol and Roger wished Katie and Will a Merry Christmas and headed up to bed, looking entirely worn out.

Yawning and stretching her arms above her head, Katie felt a familiar sleepiness creeping up on her, too.

"I had a wonderful Christmas," she said softly, staring at the Christmas tree while the fireplace crackled. "Did you?"

Will kissed her head. "The best I've ever had."

"You're not just saying that? I mean, you gave me pearls and diamond earrings and an entire spa package—"

"That was slightly selfish on my part. It's a couple's spa package, so I get the benefit of it, too."

"The point is, all I got you was a corny t-shirt that says you're the best boyfriend ever."

"And I'm going to wear it proudly. I told you I'd love it."

Katie groaned and covered her face. "Just so you know, I'm the worst gift giver ever, if that wasn't already apparent."

Will chuckled. "No, you're not. You already gave me the best gift I could have asked for."

"Right. What could a girl like me get a billionaire hunk that he doesn't already have?"

Will ran his fingers along her jawline and drew her lips to his. The kiss started softly but deepened as their souls connected. Katie ran her hands down his biceps and his fingers moved the length of her spine and settled low on her back.

He stopped the kiss by cradling her cheeks in his hands. Katie swore she could see all the way into his soul through his beautiful hazel eyes.

"Katie," he said quietly, "you're what I was missing. All I've been needing and hoping for is you, so if you're wondering what I could possibly want, the answer is you. In every possible way, you're the answer to my Christmas wish."

"People have already put up their Christmas decorations!"
Katie pressed her nose against Will's passenger side window,
staring at the enormous inflatable Christmas tree and Santa
in the middle of someone's yard.

"It is December first," Will said, putting his hand over
hers.

Katie turned her hand around and wove her fingers
between his. It'd been almost exactly a year since they'd been
officially dating, but holding his hand still hadn't gotten old.

"I know, but it makes me feel like I'm behind. I haven't
even brought my Christmas tree up out of the basement."

"That's probably my fault," Will said.

He kept his eyes on the road, giving Katie a chance to
steal a look at him. How she'd gotten so lucky to land her
dream guy was beyond her, but she was so grateful things
had worked out. She could never have imagined where life
would take her. There had been heartache, but it had also
made the happy times sweeter.

"Well, yeah," Katie said sarcastically, "if you'd quit dragging me all over the country for bigwig events, then maybe I'd have time to get my holiday decorating done."

Will laughed. "Hey, you're the one who agreed to go with me. I wasn't kidding when I said I had a lot of events to show up at."

"I know. Seriously, it's been so fun. I've loved being able to travel more and to go with you is always a treat, but I also am glad to have Holly Wreath as home base."

"Yep. I don't think I knew how much I was needing small town life again. It's nice to be able to unwind without worrying if there are paparazzi outside my window, trying to take pictures of me while I'm watching TV."

"Well, it doesn't hurt that you built your house in the middle of nowhere with a fence around the whole property, complete with an intimidating gate to discourage gawkers."

"You're the one who helped me pick out that gate."

Katie playfully rolled her eyes. "I helped you pick out everything in that house. Well, me and Piper. I'm about as clueless with decorating as you are, so I guess you should be thanking her."

"Whoever. As long as you like it, that's all I care about."

"Yeah, but it's not my house. It's yours."

Will smirked and Katie wondered if there was something he meant by it. Her heart jumped excitedly in her chest while she reminded herself not to get ahead of herself. Yes, their dating life had been amazing and fulfilling, but it wasn't like she had an engagement ring on her finger. That was something she was still patiently daydreaming about.

They drove past a maternity store and Katie jumped like she'd sat on a tack. "Oh! Speaking of Piper, did you hear?"

"Hear what?"

"She and Rudger are expecting a baby. I think she said she's due in May."

Chuckling, Will shook his head. "I've got to say, for as

quiet as Rudger is, he's not one to wait around for much. Although, neither is Ethan. He proposed to Olivia over Thanksgiving."

Katie clapped her hand over her mouth and her eyes widened as she sat up in her seat. "You're kidding!"

"Not about marriage proposals."

"I was wondering why everyone was swarming her last week at church. I can't believe I hadn't heard yet."

"It's probably because Charlotte isn't in town to feed you all the juicy gossip."

Katie sat back. "That's true. I hope she's having a good time meeting Harvey's family."

"I'm sure she's having a grand old time. I just hope she's making a good impression. She can be a bit much."

Katie smacked his arm. "Be nice. Everybody loves your sister."

Will pulled into a parking spot in front of the diner where they'd first reconnected and turned off his truck. "Shall we go in and get a bite to eat?"

"You're already hungry? I'm still stuffed from breakfast."

"It must be from all the running you keep making me do. It's messed up my metabolism."

"If you're going to run a full marathon with me this coming March, you're going to thank me for pushing you in your training."

Will opened his door. "Maybe I should cheerlead for you from the sidelines."

"Nice try." Katie opened the door and hopped out. "Let's go get you some lunch so you don't lose your resolve to keep running with me."

Inside the diner, the lunch crowd had packed every single booth and table, so they agreed to sit at the counter. A single red rose was in a vase, right between their two seats.

Katie sat on her chair and leaned over to smell the flower.

"Isn't that a nice touch?" She looked around and down the counter. "I wonder why no one else has one."

"What can I get you two lovebirds?" the waitress asked, her pen and notepad at the ready.

Will didn't bother touching the menu. "How about we start with dessert. Do you happen to have any sugar cream pie?"

"You're in luck. Today we do," the waitress said, slipping her pen and pad in her apron pocket.

Katie arched an eyebrow. "When did they get sugar cream pie on the menu?" Will shrugged and Katie noticed that same cryptic smile on his face that made her weak in the knees. "What's going on? I have a feeling you're up to something."

The waitress came back from the kitchen and set two slices of pie down in front of them. "Enjoy."

Will dug in but when Katie looked at her piece, there was an enormous, glittering diamond ring sitting on top. With trembling hands, she picked it up and inspected it. "What's this?"

Without answering directly, Will got off his chair and got down on one knee. Taking Katie's hands in his, she noticed his were quivering, too.

"Katie Holloway, I know this might seem like an unconventional location to propose, but I wanted to bring you back to the first place where I knew you and I were going to end up together. Since I first came back to town last December, I was struck by the beautiful, intelligent woman you'd become. I'm forever grateful that you've stuck with me, despite what a dope I can be sometimes. I have always felt like I'm my best version of myself when I have you with me. I love you and want to continue this journey through life at your side. Would you do me the honor of becoming my wife?"

Katie paused, watching Will through a veil of happy tears,

not because she was unsure, but because she couldn't believe it was finally happening. Sliding off her chair, she wrapped her arms around his neck and buried her face next to him.

"Yes!"

The entire diner erupted with applause and it was only then that she realized half the patrons were her friends and Will's family. Charlotte had been hiding out in a corner with Harvey, covering their faces with ballcaps, and Roger and Carol came out of the kitchen, where they'd been spying from the cook's window.

Will helped her to her feet. "I have another question for you."

"Whatever it is, my answer's yes." She let the tears streak down her cheeks as he slipped the solitaire diamond ring on her finger.

"Are you sure? You don't even know what I'm going to ask."

"I trust you."

"Alright, then let's go to the chapel."

Will took her hand, but Katie's feet rooted in place. "What?"

"I was going to ask you if you minded getting married today. Since you said yes, we're going to the chapel to get married."

"Today? But we can't. I don't have a dress, the preacher might be busy, I want all of our friends and family there—"

Will kissed her cheek reassuringly. "Already taken care of. I've been planning it for months, the whole time worrying you'd laugh in my face and tell me no."

Laughing, Katie threw her arms around his neck again, letting him twirl her around. "I could never tell you no. This is...I don't even have words...I can't believe this is happening."

"Let's not keep our guests waiting."

Will swept her out to the truck and she alternated between crying and laughing as they led a caravan of cars to the little white chapel where the parking lot was already filled. Flowers and garland were wrapped around the railing and a beautiful arch welcomed everyone into the building. A stretch limo was parked off to the side and Katie's insides trembled, wondering where they were going on their honeymoon.

She waited for Will to come around to the side to open her door. There was so much to take in that her knees felt unreliable. She leaned on Will as he led her to the front door. Inside, she was swept away by Charlotte to a room where there was an army of women ready to help her get dressed.

On a dress form, Katie recognized her mother's wedding dress with a few modifications. Charlotte noticed her staring. "I hope you don't mind. I snuck into your house again."

"I'm going to have to move that key to keep you from surprising me," Katie said as Charlotte sat her down in a chair, brushing out her hair so she could style it.

"You're not going to live there much longer anyway. Unless you wanted Will to move to your house instead of you moving to his. And guess what, I already know the passcode to get into his house, so good luck getting rid of me."

"When did you get back?" Katie asked. "I thought you were going to be with Harvey's parents for the week."

"We did have a nice visit, but we flew in last night. You think I'd miss my best friend's wedding? Who also happens to be marrying my brother? Nope."

Katie noticed a framed picture of her parents on the table where Charlotte had set her mirror. It was another special touch that brought tears to her eyes. "I love what you did with my mother's dress. It's perfect."

"It was actually Piper's idea, so thank her. She took care of getting the seamstress to get it just right."

Just then, Piper walked in the room in a lovely, silk gown. Her baby bump was already showing and she glowed with happiness. "What can I do to help?"

Charlotte gave orders to everyone and not a single person sat down until Katie's hair and makeup was done, and she was being zipped into her wedding gown. It fit like a glove.

Piper handed her a bouquet of red carnations and stems of holly leaves and berries, spilling over with baby's breath.

"Thank you," Katie said, drawing Piper in for a hug.

"So happy to have been able to help."

Heather and Oliva popped in to peek at the bride before she walked down the aisle. Like Piper, Olivia radiated happiness. It probably had something to do with the classic yet generous diamond ring she had on her own finger. Ethan had done an excellent job.

"Katie! I get to be your flower girl!" Heather spun to show off her dress and jumped up and down, barely able to contain her own excitement.

"You're an absolute doll." Katie touched one of her ringlet curls that were undoubtedly Charlotte's signature. "I couldn't have picked a better girl. Thank you for doing it for me, Heather."

"I'm just here to see when you'll be ready, so I can pass along the word to the string quartet," Olivia said.

"There's a string quartet?" Katie gasped, holding her hand to her chest. "Of course there is. Will pulled out all the stops, didn't he?"

"With Heather's and my help," Charlotte said. "If we left it completely up to him, the best you might have gotten was a recording of *Canon in D*."

Katie hugged Charlotte and Heather simultaneously. "You're the best. I can't believe you kept all of this from me!"

"I know!" Charlotte dramatically wiped her brow. "I might have exploded if it weren't for Harvey. At least I could talk his ear off about wedding stuff. Plus, I think it might have planted a few seeds in his mind about marriage."

"You think he'll ever be brave enough to ask you? I mean, it took him an entire, what? Seven months to work up the courage to ask you to the Christmas Social?" Katie said with a laugh.

"Well, maybe I'll do the asking, then. We're in an amazing day and age. Either way, don't think I'll be forgetting all this hard work I put in for you," Charlotte said. "You'd better believe I'm calling in that favor when I need you to be my maid of honor."

"Matron," Olivia corrected. "She'd actually be your matron of honor since she'll be a married woman."

Charlotte's mouth dropped like the news was hitting her for the first time. "That's right! I hadn't even thought about that. Duh, you'll be a married woman by then."

"She'll be a married woman in less than an hour," Piper interjected.

"Can we go now?" Heather asked, bouncing impatiently. "I'm so excited to toss the flowers I can't hardly stand it!"

Katie nodded. "Of course. We shouldn't keep anyone waiting, including you. I'm ready whenever you are."

In another flurry of motion, everyone took their places out in the hallway. From the back of the line, Katie could hear the music start. Heather must have been walking down the aisle when Katie heard a collective aww and, one by one, Charlotte and Piper left, leaving only Katie to walk down the aisle.

Roger was there to meet her as a stand in for Katie's late father. He was as good as a dad to her and Katie couldn't imagine better in-laws than the Ryans. They'd welcomed her into their home with open arms long before Will had.

At the head of the chapel, Will looked positively

debonaire in his tux. A single carnation was pinned to his lapel and he rocked on his heels, a nervous tick Katie had learned to look for at events when he was feeling over-whelmed. He always stopped when she reached for his hand, like she was the lifeline he needed to keep grounded. Will had always made her feel special that way, like her mere presence meant the world to him.

When Will laid eyes on Katie in her wedding attire with her veil over her face, his expression became one of awe. Katie's heart was already racing—in her wildest dreams, she couldn't have guessed this was how her day would turn out. She felt like she was living in the best sort of fantasy, where everything was perfect and nothing but happiness and love existed.

She smiled at Heather, who had her hand on Ethan's knee, and in the row in front of them, Rudger gave her a subtle nod of his head, his own personal greeting. He rested his hand on the back of the pew and his wedding ring glinted in the light. So many fairytale happily-ever-afters in Holly Wreath.

Katie knew there were other people there, but her eyes focused on Will. His nervous grin had been replaced by a full-out smile that made his whole countenance glow. When Roger handed her over to Will, he went to sit with Carol, who was already wiping tears from her eyes. Will delicately draped the veil behind her head and traced one hand down her cheek and to her jaw. He was staring at her lips.

Moving his gaze up to her eyes, he kissed her hand and whispered for only her to hear. "Are you sure you want to marry me? Here? Now?"

Holding his hand even tighter, she nodded, wondering if she might burst with happiness as it rippled through her from head to toe. "I can't think of a better way to start the most wonderful time of the year than starting our life together by marrying you."

Looking for your next billionaire series? Look for The Billionaire Needs a Wife *on Amazon!*

WILL'S SECRET SUGAR CREAM PIE RECIPE

1 deep dish pie crust, room temperature
¼ cup cornstarch
¾ cup sugar
4 Tablespoons butter + additional 4 Tablespoons, melted
2 ¼ cups heavy cream
1 Tablespoon vanilla
¼ cup cinnamon sugar
½ teaspoon nutmeg

Preheat oven to 325F. Place Pie crust in a lightly greased nine-inch pie pan, set on a baking sheet. Bake approximately 10-12 minutes or until partially baked. Meanwhile, in a medium saucepan, mix together the cornstarch and sugar until blended. Add four tablespoons melted butter and the heavy cream, stirring over medium heat until it's thick and creamy. Stir in the vanilla. Pour the mixture into the prepared pie crust and smooth out the top. Drizzle with the remaining melted butter and sprinkle evenly with the cinnamon sugar and nutmeg. Bake approximately 25 minutes, then turn on the broiler for about one minute, watching carefully to avoid burning. Remove the pie from the oven and allow to come to room temperature before refrigerating. Allow at least one hour to set. Store leftovers in the fridge. Enjoy!

ABOUT RACHAEL

Humor. Romance. Happily Ever Afters. So much to write, so little time!

USA Today Bestselling Author Rachael Eliker is an avid reader and author with eclectic tastes, but as long as the story has humor, swoony romance, and maybe a horse or two, she's happy. When she's not writing, she's probably running lonely stretches of country road, riding her old horse, or working on a home improvement project. She enjoys passing the time with her husband and children on their Indiana hobby farm, having a good laugh, and making memories with friends and family most of all.

Learn more about Rachael Eliker and her upcoming works by visiting: www.RachaelEliker.com

MORE BY THE AUTHOR

Want more billionaires? Look for Rachael's new sweet romance series, To Love a Billionaire.

For a full list of Rachael's works, search for her on Amazon.

To leave a much-appreciated review for this book, please consider writing one on your preferred platform.